THE MEANING OF
MAGGIE

A NOVEL BY
MEGAN JEAN SOVERN

chronicle books · san francisco

First Chronicle Books LLC paperback edition, published in 2015.
Originally published in hardcover in 2014 by Chronicle Books LLC.

ISBN 978-1-4521-2876-4

The Library of Congress has cataloged the original edition as follows:

Sovern, Megan Jean, author.
The meaning of Maggie / by Megan Jean Sovern.
pages cm
Summary: Eleven-year-old Maggie Mayfield is an A-plus student
with big plans for herself, but at this moment she is also facing a
lot of problems—like starting middle school and figuring out how
to help her father who is out of work and in a wheelchair.
ISBN 978-1-4521-1021-9 (alk. paper)
1. Fathers and daughters—Juvenile fiction. 2. Families—Juvenile fiction.
3. Multiple sclerosis—Juvenile fiction. 4. Middle schools—Juvenile fiction.
[1. Fathers and daughters—Fiction. 2. Family life—Fiction. 3. Multiple
sclerosis—Fiction. 4. Middle schools—Fiction. 5. Schools—Fiction.] I. Title.

PZ7.S7304Me 2014
813.6—dc23
2013029644

Manufactured in China.

Design by Amelia Mack.
Typeset in Filosofia.

10 9 8 7 6 5 4 3 2 1

Chronicle Books LLC
680 Second Street, San Francisco, California 94107
www.chroniclekids.com.

For my freckled mother, my hot sisters, and
my father who always wanted to be famous.

PROLOGUE

Beep.

Beep.

Beep.

My dad won't stop beeping.

And it's impossible to concentrate while my dad is beeping. He's been beeping for almost a whole day now. And it's not the friendly beep of the ice cream truck backing up after you chased it halfway down the block either. It's a slow beep that makes me really sleepy. But it's impossible to sleep because the chair in this hospital room is harder than the hardest substance on earth, which I know is diamond because it was on my science final two months ago, which I got a 100 on, but whatever.

It's just Dad and me in the hospital room right now. My sisters and my mom are downstairs in the cafeteria. Mom put me in charge of Dad until she gets back, which makes sense because I am way more responsible than my sisters even though they're in high school and I'm in middle school, but you know, hot girls take longer to mature.

And since I'm so responsible, I know that I'm not supposed to push or touch ANYTHING even if it looks like it'd be really fun to push or touch. And I'm keeping an extra close eye on Dad. He just fell back asleep. But I'm kind of hoping he'll wake up soon so we can split this Little Debbie. Normally I'd just eat the whole thing myself, but I figure he could use a little pick-me-up.

I'm not worried. Dad is going to be a-okay. Even Mom said so. And even though she works full time and takes care of Dad full time and fixes dinner full time and raises the three of us to be ladies full time, she's always right full time too. She's a very busy lady but even at her busiest, she's still at her best.

Like yesterday, she remembered to bring my birthday present to the hospital even though she shouldn't have because big deal things were happening. But of course she remembered and of course it was the most perfect gift ever. She gave me the most beautiful leather-bound journal and I have to use it to write something really important. And I've decided that important thing will be my memoir.

If you don't know, a memoir is a piece of autobiographical writing that examines the meaning of the author's life during a specific moment in time. I'm writing about my eleventh year on this earth because it was the most important year of my WHOLE life.

Because last year was the year that changed every-thing. It was one of those years you learn about in history class and the teacher says, "This was a year that changed EVERYTHING" and you roll your eyes and think, "Yeah right, you said that last chapter." But by the time you reach the end of the chapter, you realize you've high-lighted every single word because every single word was really important. That's how last year felt for me. Like the entire thing was highlighted.

And that's why I'm writing this memoir. Because just like any other future president of the United States of America, I have a story worth telling. So maybe I didn't cut down a cherry tree and maybe I don't have wooden teeth and I wasn't born in a log cabin with a dirt floor and nine thousand brothers and sisters. I still have something to say. And that's why I'm writing this for prosperity or posterity or propensity, all of which I will look up once we get home.[1] And well, I'm writing this because when visiting hours are over, I'll be back in the waiting room with nothing to do but stare at the vending machine full of M&M's that Mom says I've had enough of.

Mom would want me to start this whole thing by being brave and pulling up my bootstraps. Whenever big deal

---

1.   If we ever get home.

stuff happens in our family (and a lot of big deal things happen), Mom tells us to "pull up our bootstraps" even though we live in Georgia and most of the time it's too hot to wear boots, but pulling up your shoelaces just sounds weird.

So I'm going to do just that. And it turns out, I'm more prepared to write this memoir than I even realized. I've been doing research pretty much all year without even knowing it. There were all the times I hid behind the couch while my sister Tiffany got in trouble. And all the times I listened in on my other sister Layla's phone calls. And all of the glasses I put up to my parents' door to decode their secret mumbles. I wouldn't need the glass at all but my ears aren't top notch. I blame it on all the loud rock 'n' roll music my parents listened to while I was both in and outside of the womb.

Up until last year Dad worked and Mom did mom things and my sisters did big sister things like totally ignore me. But then Dad's legs fell all the way asleep.

His legs had been in and out of sleep for a few years. Sometimes they would wake up and he would walk with a cane. But his cane has been in the closet for a while now and I don't think it's coming out. It's like his legs are in the deepest sleep ever. It's like they've been hypnotized by David Copperfield[2] and no amount of snapping or clapping will wake them up. And now on top of

---

2. The magician, not the Dickens character.

sleeping legs, he's also really sick and that's why we're here with the beeping. The unfriendly non-ice-cream-truck really scary beeping.

I'm feeling about a million things at this moment. And I guess the only thing I'm not feeling now is hungry because I just ate that entire Little Debbie even though I double swore to myself that I'd wait until Dad woke up to share it. But I couldn't help it. I'm tired. I slept on a floor last night. In a hospital waiting room. Next to my sister who kicked the dickens out of me with her perfect legs all night long.

And not getting my usual full eight hours of REM sleep hasn't helped my exhaustion, both physical and emotional. Physical exhaustion because of the floor. I feel like I pulled an all-nighter at the factory like David Copperfield.[3] And emotional exhaustion because it's so hard and weird to see Dad so sick. Yeah he's in a wheel-chair, but he also eats an apple a day to keep the doctor away. But I guess something snuck past that last apple because nurses keep coming in and out of Dad's room. And they keep poking him with needles and taking his temperature and changing these big bags of medicine and listening to his heart. I bet if they listened with their ears instead of a stethoscope they'd hear it say, "I'm fine. Let me go home and stop scaring my family. Especially Maggie. Because she's

---

3. The Dickens character, not the magician.

my favorite. That's right, Maggie's my favorite. Not Layla like everyone thinks."

But everything will be okay. Dad *will* get better. That's what tough guys do. But still, I have to admit I'm worried. And it's that deep-down-in-your-guts worried that's impossible to get rid of no matter how many Mike and Ikes you eat.

I guess I'm starting to realize that being brave isn't so black and white. It isn't something you either are or aren't. It isn't an absolute. Because you can run out of bravery. Your metaphorical bravery tank can run dry. But it's up to you to fill it back up again. To muster all the courage you can. To pull up your bootstraps. And no one does this better than Dad. And he doesn't even wear boots because he doesn't need boots because his feet never touch the ground.

I never knew I would need so much bravery until everything changed a full year before yesterday. A full year before Dad started beeping. It was my eleventh birthday. And it started with another noise just as annoying as the beep. It began with a buzz.

CHAPTER ONE

BUZZ!

My alarm clock went off at seven A.M.

I hit the snooze button.

BUZZ!

I hit the snooze button again.

BUZZ!

Third time's the charm, right?

One of Tiffany's giant giraffe legs kicked me in the shin. Ouch! "Okay, okay! It's off!"

She kicked me again. "Stop setting the alarm! It's summer!"

God, she was so impossible.

So I yelled, "God, you're so impossible!"

She had no idea that if you slept in over the summer it would be twice as hard to get back to the grind once school started. I couldn't believe I shared a room with such an underachiever. I wrote my parents, like, a million letters begging them to let me live in the garage. I didn't need heat or air. My body temperature naturally regulated. But they didn't believe me. They didn't—

BUZZ!

Ah, curse word!

I shielded myself from another kick. "I swear I turned it off!"

Tiffany gave me the evil eye. "You're SO dead."

I glared back at her. "Be nice to me. It's my birthday."

IT WAS MY BIRTHDAY! With all the buzzing and yelling and kicking I'd almost forgotten it was my birthday! Eleven years old. The beginning of everything! One year closer to college. One year closer to voting. One year closer to getting a tattoo, not that I wanted to get a tattoo. They're terrifying. But it was nice knowing I was closer to getting one anyway.

I pulled on my overalls, ran to the mirror, and ta-da!

Oh no.

Oh dear.

Oh gosh.

I looked the same as I did when I was ten.

Maybe Tiffany could spot a difference. "Hey Tiffany, do I look any different?"

She rolled over and gave me a look. "Yeah. You look even nerdier than you did yesterday." She swung her other giraffe leg out from under the covers, pushed me into the hallway, and slammed the door.

In my face.

I yelled, "You're gonna be sorry!" Then I heard a loud mechanical thud against the door. Good-bye, alarm clock.

But don't worry, I wasn't going to let any of this ruin my big day. What if growing older and wiser took a day to take? Maybe my first wrinkle would surface soon. So I gave my hair a tousle and reached for the boom box because nothing says "It's my birthday!" better than a "Hail to the Chief" processional down the hallway. I pushed Play and marched into the dining room for the best part of any best day: GIFTS.

Dad saluted me but didn't stand because, well, Dad doesn't stand. I saluted him back and couldn't help but notice the gigantic envelope waiting for me on the table.

"Happy birthday, Mags. You look so much older. More distinguished."

"Thanks, I've been working on it," I said. I poured myself a mug of OJ. "Hey Dad, is that what I think it is?"

"If you think it's the autographed picture of Susan B. Anthony you asked for last year, then no. She still hasn't responded to my letter."

"I'm not surprised. She's been dead for eighty-two years."

Dad laughed. "Well, that explains a lot." I was pretty sure he was joking. "Hopefully I was more successful this year."

He slid the envelope across the table toward me and my hands shook.

I couldn't believe it. I had asked him to buy me stock in Coca-Cola[4] for my birthday and he'd actually done it.

I pulled the paper out of the envelope, which was manila because important things come in manila envelopes. The certificate was fancy and official and said I had three whole shares of stock IN MY NAME. Coca-Cola was a blue-chip stock too, which meant it made more money than most, which meant I was going to be a millionaire.[5]

I wasn't just Maggie Mayfield, the girl, anymore. I was Maggie Mayfield, member of a carbonated dynasty! It no longer mattered that Mom never allowed me to drink it, now I owned it! I bet you get to drink all the Coke you want at the annual shareholders' meeting!

Dad took the certificate from my excited hands. "I'll put this away for safekeeping, okay?"

"Wait! Let me show Mom first!" I dashed into the kitchen past the sink overflowing with dishes, past the empty cinnamon roll pan, and past the almost bad bananas.

"Mother," I announced. "I'm rich."

----

4. During a Sunday marathon of *Lifestyles of the Rich and Famous*, I decided it was about time I got rich and famous. When I asked Dad about making fast cash, he suggested the stock market. So I researched stocks and decided to invest in the one thing I really believed in: sugar you can drink.

5. A millionaire!

"I'm glad one of us is." She grabbed the coffeepot and we joined Dad back in the dining room.

He was thumbing through the paper. "Remember Mags, buy low, sell high."

Mom laughed. "Do you even know what that means?"

"Of course I do. I read it in a Far Side cartoon."

"Don't worry, folks. I'm in a dividend reinvestment plan. I'm making money as we speak." I took the last swig of OJ and pushed my empty mug toward Mom with a wink.

"No coffee, Maggie."

"Come on! I'm a Wall Street tycoon! I need caffeine!"

"Nice try, but no. Now go get ready. It's almost time to go."

Mom had something pretty huge planned for my big day and that huge thing was a tour of the local newspaper. It was just the kind of behind-the-scenes action I needed to get in with the press before my presidential election. Even if my presidential election was a couple decades away.

But first things first. I needed my lucky red scarf. Sure we were in the hot and humid thick of July, but I had to have it. I never did any big deal things without it. What if all the reporters kept the newsroom below freezing so the ink wouldn't melt? What if a top-notch editor wanted me to be his girl Friday and we were off to a frozen place to cover some big deal story about a

Russian king or a Dairy Queen? I couldn't leave my lucky scarf behind.

I had saved it from the pit of Mom's closet last November while on a mission to uncover my Halloween candy stash.[6] I never found the candy, but I discovered the scarf and it was definitely meant for me. And my neck.

I double-wrapped the scarf and reached for my notebook and my glasses, which were another great find from Mom's closet. They were a pair of Dad's old glasses that Mom never let me wear because she said they made me look like a cereal killer, which I didn't really understand because I loved cereal too much to kill it. I tucked the glasses into my front pocket just in case I needed to get up close and personal with some facts. And then it was "off to the presses."

We waltzed into the newsroom and I felt immediately at home among the desks and pencils and doughnuts. We met an old-school reporter named Hank who smelled like dust and deodorant. I asked him a bazillion questions like, "Are the facts cold and hard when you find them or do they need an incubation period?" and, "Should I start drinking coffee now or wait until it can't stunt my growth?" But he didn't really have any answers or maybe he did but he kept them secret because that's

6. My candy stash that mysteriously disappeared while I was in the throes of a mini Snickers mini coma.

what reporters do: They keep secrets right up until the big story breaks.

I took notes while he told us all about the beat. Busting local political corruption. Uncovering scandals plaguing Little League baseball. Announcing births and deaths ON THE SAME DAY. And promoting Atlanta businesses like my personal favorite: the Highland Bakery in the Old Fourth Ward. They have cinnamon rolls bigger than my head. And I have a really big head.

I tried to pay attention to his every word, but I couldn't keep my eyes from wandering over to his desk. No magnifying glass? No trench coat? Weird. They were probably in his car with his wiretapping kit.

At the loading dock, reporters and editors buzzed around us chatting up big deal stories while drinking big deal cups of joe.[7] None of them were wearing news caps like I had imagined but they were talking really fast about really smart things and I thought, Note to self: Find Dad's old stopwatch and try to increase my word count per minute. I was going to have to think and speak a lot faster if I was going to keep up with the fast-paced world of facts.

Hank apologized for having to rush us out the door but as a parting gift, he let me have the first paper off the

---

7.   Joe is slang for coffee. Just like java, mud, and Mom's Life Force. Well that last one isn't as much slang as it is God's honest truth.

presses at NO CHARGE. It was still warm and smelled new even though I knew the news was already old. The ink stuck to my fingers and at that moment, my life was PERFECT.

After we left, my cheeks actually hurt from smiling so much, which hadn't happened since my last birthday when Mom took me to see *Les Miserables*, which was LES AWESOME. We zoomed up the driveway and I rushed inside, but I didn't wash my hands right away. I wanted to keep the smudged facts on my hands. I wanted to keep the perfect.

I ran over to Dad's chair to show him the headlines on my hands and I found two things I didn't expect.

1) He was sitting with his legs crossed like a pretzel.[8]

2) He looked super sad.

How had he gotten this way? Both super sad and pretzel-like? And why was the stereo cranked all the way up? It was so loud it felt like an actual zeppelin was crashing through the roof. But it wasn't. It was just the band Led Zeppelin going on and on about heartbreak or Middle Earth or some other nonsense. When we'd left earlier, Dad had been all smiles and had told us to hurry back because he wanted cake, which I understood because I always wanted cake.

---

8.   This style of sitting is also known as "Indian style" but I don't call it that because it's not politically correct and "Native American style" just sounds weird.

Then it hit me.

I'd missed the biggest scoop of the day. I'd been so overwhelmed that morning I hadn't noticed something so different about Dad: He was home. Every other birthday wish from him had been a phone call from work. But he wasn't at work. Not today.

I turned the stereo down and bellied up to his chair. "Hey Dad, why aren't you at work? Is everything okay?"

He blinked a long blink. "Hey Mags, how was the newspaper? Did you love it? What was your favorite part?"

I got really serious. "Every part was my favorite part."

"That's really great. Hey, will you get your sisters for me? I'm calling a little family meeting."

A family meeting? On my birthday? But what about cake and presents and everyone giving speeches about how great I was? What kind of inauguration into being eleven was this?

"But what about my birthday?"

"It'll just take a minute. And then we'll have cake. Promise."

I took promises really seriously. Pinky-swear promises and spit-shake promises and especially promises to have cake. So I called Tiffany and Layla and they opened their doors at the same time because they're pretty much the same person. With the same brain. And the same bra size.

"What's up?" Layla asked.

"Dad wants to talk to us."

Tiffany glanced down at her hands. "Tell him I'll be there when my nails are dry."

"You better come now," I said. "It sounds important."

They followed me into the living room where Mom was now sitting next to Dad. They looked serious, really serious.

Dad cleared his throat. "Girls, your mother got a job. We should be really proud of her. She's going to be working at a big fancy hotel downtown."

This didn't make any sense.

"Why would you do that? Who's going to take care of us?" I panicked. "We'll starve to death!"

Dad answered before Mom could.

"I'm going to take care of us." He took a giant breath like it might be his last.

"I quit my job."

He said it again but this time he said it differently.

This time he said it like he was saying it to himself.

"I quit my job."

CHAPTER TWO

My brain was freaking out but my mouth didn't say a thing. I had a million questions but I didn't know which to ask first.

"Is this because you fell at work?" Layla asked.

Okay, now I had a million and one questions. "You fell at work?! Was it in the lunchroom? I did that once and it was terrible. Chocolate milk went EVERYWHERE."

Dad took Mom's hand and squeezed it. "I took a tumble in the bathroom a couple weeks ago. It was no big deal, really. But my boss and I decided it was time to think about what's next for me."

There was a long silence until Mom finally said something. "Your dad's worked so hard for so long at the airport. You know, he started out as a baggage handler and he worked his way up to gate agent. They're really going to miss him. They'll never find anyone as good to replace him."

"Then why is he leaving?" Tiffany asked.

"Because it's time," Dad said.

"Time for what?"

"Time for a new chapter," Mom answered.

Tiffany glared at Dad. "So you're going to be here, like, all the time?"

"Yep." Dad smiled.

"Great. That's just *great*." Tiffany stormed down the hall and I followed her because I liked when she got upset because her face got all weird and splotchy. She collapsed onto her bed and smooshed her face under her pillow.

"What's your deal?" I asked.

She threw the pillow on the floor.

"My life. Is. Over."

"What? Why?" I offered her an Oreo from the bag I kept under my bed.

She shooed it away. "He's going to be here like twenty-five[9] hours a day. Watching our every move."

"I don't care. All of my moves are 100% legal."

Tiffany buried her face in another pillow and then Mom knocked on our door and said it was time to eat.

No one really talked at dinner, which was unusual because someone always had a story or a joke or at

---

9. Seriously.

the very least we would watch *Jeopardy!* and guess the answers. Well, some of us guessed. Some of us[10] just knew the answers.

But tonight Mom turned the TV off before we sat down so there was mostly silence. And the silence made my tummy feel weird so I didn't really eat, which was a super bummer because it was my special birthday dinner of meatloaf and mashed potatoes.[11]

After everyone was done, Layla and Tiffany helped Mom with the dishes and I pushed Dad into the living room and locked his wheels so we could talk man to girl. Something had been bothering me and I had to know the answer.

"Were you scared when you fell? It sounds scary."

He kissed me on the forehead. "How about you fix your dear old dad a cocktail?"

I didn't push him to answer. It didn't feel right. So I headed for the fridge and stood on my tiptoes to reach the freezer. I almost had the ice when a freckled arm beat me to it.

"Can I help?" Mom asked.

"Dad wants a cocktail. Stat."

"Good. So does Mom."

Mom broke ice cubes into two glasses and mixed the formula parents love: ¾ bad stuff and ¼ Coca-Cola. She

---

10. Me.

11. Extra mashed.

carried the concoctions into the living room and then Dad started time traveling.

Dad loved telling all kinds of stories from his past, which supposedly Abraham Lincoln did a lot too. But Dad's stories weren't about history or bravery or progress. Mostly they were just about hippies and protests and details lost in crowded rock shows two thousand years ago when he was a teenager and lived downtown and raised all kinds of you-know-what.[12]

Twenty minutes in, Dad asked Mom to get "the photo album" and she disappeared down the hall and came back with a photo album covered in red and blue and green flowers. I'd never seen this album before and I could tell Layla and Tiffany hadn't either. I think we expected it to be filled with baby pictures of us or of Layla's recitals or my spelling bees, but it wasn't. When I opened the cover, a picture of Mom and Dad fell out. A really young Mom and Dad.

Mom grabbed it and yelled, "Look! Prom!"

In the picture Mom was wearing a white lace dress and Dad was wearing a tuxedo with ruffles in the ugliest shade of blue I'd ever seen.

"Ew, Dad!" Layla screeched. "What's growing on your face?"

---

12. It's a curse word that starts with an *h*, ends with two *l*s, and has an *e* in the middle. Got it?

Dad laughed. "Oh man. Those are chops. Don't they look cool?"

And for the first time in the history of time, my sisters and I agreed on something. The chops DID NOT look cool.

From what I could piece together from the photo album, this was the story of a boy with ugly chops and a girl with a million freckles. They saved all kinds of ticket stubs and flowers and matchbooks. They threw peace signs at the camera and wore shirts that were too tight and pants that were too big at the bottom. And a funny-looking leaf got its own page, which made my sisters giggle. I pretended to know why because I was eleven and when you're eleven you get inside jokes but I'd only been eleven for less than a day so it was okay that I didn't get this one just yet.

I asked Dad to tell me about it but he refused.

"I'll tell you in ten years," he promised.

I hated when he said that and he said it often. The worst part was it was always ten years no matter how old I was. Which meant instead of getting one year closer every year, I was always the same years away from ever knowing the grown-up stuff Dad didn't want me to know.

It was always infuriating and it wasn't fair and it wasn't nice and it wasn't right to keep things from your children. Unless they were really scary things like matches or poison or beets because beets tasted like dirt. I would always beg Dad to tell me things and he always swore that he would—in ten years.

Then Mom jumped on the time machine and did something she never did. She started telling us EVERY-THING. And Mom never tells us ANYTHING.

This is what she told us: She went on something called a "magical mystery tour" which was some kind of hippie spring break that lasted more than a week. It included, but was not limited to:

1. Hitchhiking across the country, which you should never do because you will get killed, but Mom didn't because it was a "different time."
2. Screaming into the Grand Canyon to hear her ECHO, ECHO, echo.
3. Wearing flowers in her hair in San Francisco.
4. And almost getting a tattoo in Chicago.
   a. A TATTOO.
   b. EXCLAMATION POINT.
   c. EXCLAMATION POINT.
   d. EXCLAMATION POINT.

Evidently, once she solved all of the magical mysteries, she found her way back below the Mason-Dixon and met Dad. He asked her to be his girl forever and they got married and it was all happily ever after. But then the fun pictures ended as the '80s began and I guess that made sense because that's when Dad's arms and legs started falling asleep.

Mom and Dad didn't say so in the family meeting, but I knew the real reason he left work was because his legs just wouldn't wake all the way back up. I had overheard them talking about it one night while I'd been following a lead on a piece of cheesecake. I'd heard Dad's voice dive into a whisper. "It's only a matter of time before my legs are gone for good."

I couldn't believe it! Dad's legs were permanently falling asleep?! I'd panicked in secret while quietly opening the fridge door. And then, just when I'd needed it most, I'd discovered something else terrible. Someone had eaten all the cheesecake.

But all of that was a million miles away from our living room as Dad's spirits flowed and lifted. He seemed so happy as he relived his wayward youth, story by story. I tried to relate, but I just couldn't.

"I can't believe you all had so much fun being young. I just want to be old. I want to be old and rich and smell like butterscotch."

You would have thought I'd said something super awful. Like that I hated Led Zeppelin. Or worse, that I was a Republican. Dad unfolded his feet, let down his legs, and pulled my face to his.

"Can't you see how you have the whole world in front of you, Maggie?"

First of all, that's not even possible because just as much of the world is in front of me as is behind me because that's just how geography works.

He could tell I was skeptical. "There's a lot of 'what ifs' in life, Mags. You owe it to yourself to see what's out there. You know every president takes a different path."

I considered it. What if one day I hitchhiked across the country? Nope. Too many ax murderers. What if one day I took a plane out west? Maybe. I did like to fly because when you fly you get to chew gum even though it rots your teeth. What if my Magic Markers made protest posters? I did have a lot to protest, both related to Tiffany and unrelated to Tiffany. What if I had friends with dreams and VW buses? Sure, that sounded cooler than friends with regular buses. What if one day I grew my hair so long every strand told a different story? That sounded really cool. Although too bad my face was so round. I could never have long hair. At least that's what Tiffany said.

I was really starting to get confused. That morning I'd known exactly what I wanted. I wanted to be president and I wanted to be rich, not necessarily in that order. But now Dad was making it seem like there was more to life than all of that, WHICH WAS NEWS TO ME.

I'd always thought that all the answers to life's questions were in books. I'd thought knowing where the sidewalk ended and where the red fern grew and where the wild things were could help me figure out LIFE. But maybe Dad was right. What if I needed to write my own story? I closed my eyes and the weight of the world settled on my eyelids. And when I opened them, I realized my legs were also crossed like a pretzel.

My head was going to explode. Plus, I was up way past my school night/summer vacation bedtime.

"I can't deal with all this possibility at once. So I will bid you farewell, family." I tipped my pretend cap toward Dad. "Until tomorrow, good sir."

I headed down the hall for some well-earned rest when Mom called after me, "What about your cake?"

I turned around. She was holding the chocolate-on-chocolate cake I'd begged for with eleven yellow candles burning just for me. As much as I wanted to retire for the evening, it was my civic duty to make a wish. And while there wasn't any scientific evidence, I believed with all my heart that the world progressed one wish at a time. That's why while my family sang "Happy Birthday," I thought long and hard about what I wanted most in the whole wide world. And the list was long.

Should I wish newsman Hank would call me the next day and ask for a front-page interview? Should I wish for my own room like I had every single year before? Should I wish Dad's legs would wake up again? Or was that wish too big for just eleven candles? Would I have to wait for that one until I was older, when I had more wish power?

There were too many wishes to consider. So I took a deep breath and wished for the wish that jumped fastest to the front of my mind.

CHAPTER THREE

I wished school was all year 'round!

And even though my dream didn't come true, September arrived and before I knew it, the first bell of the school year rang. The first bell of the school year was probably my favorite sound ever. And this first bell was even more special because I was in a whole new school in a whole new grade with whole new kids. It was a new beginning, a blank slate, a manifest destiny. My heart raced and not just because I was running late because my locker was jammed with encyclopedias D through F, which I had brought with me JUST IN CASE. My heart raced because I was totally enveloped in the thrilling pursuit of KNOWLEDGE.

Middle school was super fancy compared to elementary school especially since they'd done away with that waste of learning time called recess. Which was why sixth grade was definitely going to be my most knowledgeable grade yet.

My first class of the day was English which would be a breeze because I'd already read most of the required reading over the summer. Reading the books a second time would be just for pleasure.

Second-period Advanced History got my blood pumping as Mrs. Nicol assigned an eight-page paper due at the end of the semester, which was going to be my greatest paper writing feat yet. And I already knew what my subject was going to be: the first woman Supreme Court justice, Sandra Day O'Connor. I loved Sandra Day O'Connor mostly because she was super smart and partly because she wore a robe all the time and that seemed both regal and comfy.

In third-period Advanced Science, we picked out our goggles for the year and I chose a pair with an extra-long strap to accommodate my brain getting bigger and bigger. Fourth-period Advanced Math was all about percentages and I 100% loved it. And lunch was the best ever because I got a whole table all to myself so I spread out my notebooks and went to town on a stack of syllabi. By the time I finished my PB&J, zebra cakes, and fruit snacks, I'd also finished writing down every important due date in my datebook and highlighting them in their correlating subject colors.

French was *très magnifique*. We picked our French

names for the year and I chose Marie after Marie Antoinette because she let people eat cake. And study hall was productive and perfect. I sharpened all my pencils and assigned all my notebook dividers and OH MY GOODNESS WHO IS THAT.

The most beautiful boy I'd ever seen sat down in front of me. Or maybe he wasn't beautiful but he was definitely cute. You know, cute for a boy who wasn't a dignitary or royalty or something.

My palms started to sweat, which usually only happened during Quiz Bowl lightning rounds. I wasn't really sure what was happening. But I liked it and hated it in equal parts.

I peered over his shoulder and saw the name Clyde scribbled on his notebook. I didn't know this kid. Sure, I didn't know a lot of kids on the first day of middle school. But it didn't seem like he was from another elementary school. It seemed like he was from another planet. Another galaxy. Another universe. Maybe he was an alien? Impossible. Aliens weren't that good looking.

I locked eyes with his feet and tried not to stare even though my eyeballs really wanted to. He wore black-and-white Converse sneakers filthy with grass stains and in black marker he'd written "Neil Young" on the bottom of his right sole. Weird. His mismatched socks led to skinny legs that led to cutoff corduroy shorts that led to a skeleton T-shirt that led to his hazel eyes looking right at me. Oh dear.

He leaned in. "Hey, do you know today's date?"

I fumbled a couple "ums" and then Idiot[13] Oswald said something that ruined my life.

"Hey Maggie. You better answer him because that's the only time you'll ever get asked for a date."

The class snickered and I died. Seriously, if someone were writing a book about me, my last words on earth would've been "September sixth, 1988."

I shrank into my seat but Clyde defended my honor— my honor!—which no one had ever defended before.

"Hey, I wasn't talking to you." He smiled RIGHT AT ME. "I was talking to Maggie."

HOW DID HE KNOW MY NAME? I died again. Seriously, I died twice in one day.

After school I ran home from the bus stop as fast as I could which wasn't very fast because my book bag weighed as much as a baby rhinoceros. The wheels in my head were moving way faster than my feet. Why did Jeff Oswald have to ruin the most perfect of perfect days? Why didn't Jeff Oswald's mother swallow him at birth? Why did the cute boy ask me for the date when he could have asked anyone? And why did looking at him make me want to lose my lunch when I love lunch more than anything?

Could it be? Was I in love with Clyde? Did I even have time for love? I just had so many other things going on

---

13. Real name: Jeff.

like school and homework and I had big plans to start a Model UN club and so far I was the only member so I had to represent every country at the same time. Of course I didn't have time for love! I mean, what did love even feel like? Sure my pulse was all over the place but that seemed normal for the first day of school. And my palms did sweat when I saw him but maybe that was because my hands were super excited for my new school year pencils. I didn't know if I felt like I was in love. Yet I didn't have any scientific evidence to the contrary. What was I going to do?

I thought about all the great love stories throughout history. Romeo and Juliet. Peanut butter and jelly. Mom and Dad. All of them fell in love when they were young just like me. My parents met when they were sixteen, which was only five years older than me and I was a mature eleven too. I took vitamins and read the paper and I owned stock.

Maybe it was time for me to take a gentleman friend. But I had a lot of work ahead if I was going to make this happen. There was no way a cool kid like Clyde would like a girl like me. Sure, you could call me a lot of things: Gifted. Presidential. Genius. But I was far from cool. To be honest, being cool had never really interested me. But now, I needed to get cool FAST. And there was only one person I knew who could make me cool: Dad.

Dad and I had only talked about boys once before when he said something about birds and bees and then he told me it was just natural and I asked what was just natural and he said s-e-x and I'd freaked out, run to my room, slammed the door, and watched PBS for three hours just so I could feel wholesome again. Hopefully, the conversation about Clyde would go better.

So just as the five o'clock news ended and just before the six o'clock news began, I walked into the living room, cleared my throat, and swallowed my fear.

"Dad?"

He answered without looking away from the TV. "You can't have any money."

"I don't want any money." I took an Oreo from the stash next to him, twisted it open, and gave him half. It was the cream side too—our favorite.

"The cream side? This must be serious. What's going on, Mags?"

I confessed how I thought I *might* be in love with this new boy named Clyde who looked like an Outsider, cute like Ponyboy, but mysterious like Sodapop. Who scribbled pictures of guitars and airplanes in his notebook and on his tennis shoes. Oh and he was really into Neil Young, just like Dad. Or at least into Neil Young enough that he would write his name on his shoe. Why would he do that? Mom would kill me if I wrote on my shoes.

Dad interrupted. "Whoa whoa whoa. Maggie, you're breaking my heart—"

He understood!

"I know! I can't believe it either. I'm in love!"

"I can't believe you don't understand why he's into Neil Young."

WHAT!

"Dad! You're totally missing the point!"

"Calm down, I get it. But first things first. Push me over to my records."

I locked his wheels in front of the stereo and handed him a giant stack of records. He thumbed past a naked lady holding an airplane, past a blimp on fire, past a "Greetings from Asbury Park" postcard, and finally stopped on a sun behind the words *Harvest Neil Young*. His fingers were sleepy, so I pulled the record from the sleeve, set it on the turntable, and lowered the needle. There was a loud crackle, a pop, and a few more rice krispy noises. Then an acoustic guitar met a harmonica and made music.

As we listened, I felt my heart rate lowering and before I knew it my head was bobbing with Dad's. That night, I understood Neil Young. I understood why he was on the bottom of Clyde's sole. And I'll never forget when he sang softly about being a miner searching for a heart of gold.

On the third song, Dad turned Neil down and lifted my chin up. "Okay, Maggie. Number one. Keep that chin up. Boys like confidence. They don't know they do, but trust me, they do."

I understood. Sort of.

"Love can make you do crazy things." Dad smiled. "And I should know. I did a lot of crazy things for your mom."

He started time traveling. "On our first date, I showed up walking on my hands. I just knew it would blow her away. But I never thought her dad would answer the door. But he did and when it creaked open, all I saw were old man loafers."

He'd toppled over and Grandpa didn't look pleased and Dad was all kinds of embarrassed and his heart was in his throat and he couldn't believe he'd thought walking on his hands was a good idea. He had just needed to be more confident.

Dad turned Neil back up and shouted, "This is where it gets GOOD!" A really pretty sounding harmonica blared from the speakers and we listened and listened some more. On the fourth song, Dad turned the music down just a little.

"I hope you know it's okay if you like a boy. And it's definitely okay to be confused. A lot of great things come out of confusion. Like great music. And great love. And it sounds like this kid is cool. It also wouldn't hurt if he came from a significant amount of family money."

"Dad, do you think I'm cool? Cool enough for a cool boy to like me back?"

"You'd be a lot cooler if you liked Neil Young. So, do you?"

"I guess so," I said. "It's no symphony of The Planets. But his voice is nice."

"Ha. Okay. Well, I think you're really cool, Mags. Always have."

I hugged my arms around his chair. "Cooler than Tiffany?"

He lowered his voice. "Oh yeah. Way cooler."

Mom let us listen through dinner but halfway through "Old Man" she lifted the needle off the record. "Okay, time for bed you two."

"Oh, come on," Dad begged. "Let us listen a little longer."

"No way, I know what's next. You're going to make her listen to Deep Purple and then she's going to sleep in our bed for a month like when you made her listen to Black Sabbath."

"That happened one time!" I objected.

Mom wasn't budging. "It's late. Time to put the records away."

I picked up the stack of records from Dad's lap and put them *gently* back in the sleeve just like he said. Then I followed Mom as she pushed Dad back to their bedroom. His arms were extra sleepy so she brushed his teeth and I gave him a glass of water to gargle. Then she combed his hair because he needed his hair to look perfect even when he was sleeping.

I pushed him next to the bed, locked his wheels, and held the chair as Mom leaned down to pick him up. She pulled his sleeping arms around her neck and on the count of one, two, three, she stood up with Dad in her arms. She was just about to lower him into bed when he shouted.

"Wait!"

Mom looked worried. "What's wrong?"

Dad laughed. "Look. We're dancing."

Mom laughed with him and they swayed together until her back and knees couldn't hold him anymore. She lowered him into bed and I pulled the blankets up to his chin and wished him good night even though most of his body was already asleep.

Dad reached for Mom's hand. "Thanks for the dance, my dear."

Mom kissed him on the cheek. "Anytime."

She picked up the remote and searched for the nine o'clock news and Dad looked over at me all googly-eyed. "See, Maggie. Love isn't so bad."

Mom looked interested. "Wait a second, Maggie. Are you in love?"

"It's not like that." My face felt hot. "He barely knows I'm alive."

"You'll have to tell me all about him sometime. How about tomorrow, sweetie? When I'm not so tired." Mom smiled.

"You're always too tired."

She kissed me good night. "Tomorrow, I promise."

She closed the door and I went to bed with her promise and "Heart of Gold" stuck in my head and heart.

The next day at school, I was all nerves when I took my seat in study hall. Clyde ran to his chair just as the warning bell rang and I quickly opened my faded copy of *The Outsiders* as a hint that I was totally down with his people. He opened his notebook and shaded in a wing on one of his airplane sketches. I had to get his attention, so I started humming softly. He turned around with one eyebrow up.

"'Heart of Gold'? I love that song."

I remembered Dad's advice and played it super cool. "Me too." I looked away the way cool girls do. "It's my favorite."

Clyde leaned back. "*Harvest* is an amazing album, but I prefer *After the Gold Rush*."

Oh no. Was this Neil Young guy an actual miner? He sure did talk about mining for hearts and gold a lot so maybe he was. I was so confused that words just fumbled out of my mouth.

"Yeah, I bet things got crazy after 1849. I mean, with all the westward expansion and dysentery and everything."

Clyde laughed. "You're funny." And then he turned back around.

Funny? I didn't want to be funny. I wanted to be cool. But I guessed funny was a start. A good start.

After school, I couldn't wait to tell Dad about my progress. I almost ran all the way home from the bus stop, swung open the door, and yelled, "Dad! Dad!"

But my yell was met with a "Shhhh! Shhh!"

Dad was watching TV on mute while Mom was fast asleep on the couch. She must have gotten off from work early. He waved me over and motioned to me to roll him to the laundry room, where a mountain of laundry was waiting to be washed.

"I just wanted to tell you about *the boy*," I whispered.

"Tell me about it while we start a load of laundry," he whispered back.

"But that's Mom's job."

Dad shook his head. "Not anymore. We're going to help her, okay? Where's the detergent?"

I stopped him and picked up the right container. "I think it's this one that says 'detergent.'"

Dad laughed quietly. "Right."

"Why are we doing this?"

He wheeled up right next to me. "Because love makes you do crazy things, remember?"

CHAPTER FOUR

Mom had become a puddle of clothes on the floor.

She was a half-eaten salad. A half-read book. A half-awake/half-asleep zombie who got home at six, fixed dinner at seven, put Dad in bed at eight and could barely keep her eyes open at nine.

Mom never yelled at Tiffany and me to clean up our room anymore but I wished she would because Tiffany's unmentionables were everywhere and I had to mention them because they were freaking me out. Actually, Mom never stopped me from doing anything anymore. She never stopped me from having ice cream for dessert. Or dinner. Or breakfast. She never even checked my homework even though there was never anything to check because I got everything right but sometimes it was just nice to hear how smart I was. But ever since she'd gone to work, Mom had become one adjective and one adjective only: tired.

And honestly, I didn't understand why. I mean yeah she got up early and yeah she worked all day. But she also drank coffee, which woke your brain up and which I wished I could drink, but no, that was the one thing she still wouldn't let me do. And she worked at a hotel which couldn't be that hard because there were beds to nap in everywhere and famous people to do famous things with. If I worked there I would have jumped up and down on beds for a few hours then I'd probably hobnob with someone like Nelson Mandela[14] and we would order room service and solve world peace over pancakes. Then I'd help Bruce Springsteen with his luggage and he'd ask where I was from, and I'd say I was "born in the USA" and we would have a good laugh because I'm hilarious. And then he would tip me five hundred dollars and I'd buy more Coca-Cola stock.

Seriously, her job sounded more like play than work. And then came Take Your Daughter to Work Day at Mom's hotel.

Usually I would have been beside myself about missing a day of school considering I didn't even miss school when I was sick, which was seldom because I took twice the recommended daily dose of Flintstones vitamins. And even when a cold snuck past Fred and Wilma, I

---

14. This guy was always on the news and Dad said he was a good guy so I liked him. I also liked him because his name sounded like a marshmallow in my mouth.

would still NEVER miss school. But this was different and I couldn't help but be excited about going to work with Mom.

I didn't give much thought to my outfit the night before. I knew I was going to spend most of the day in a cushy billion-thread-count robe lounging on billion-thread-count sheets eating billion-chocolate-count M&M's from the minibar. So I set out my overalls and a fancy cardigan (just in case I met someone famous).

Layla said she couldn't go because she had a French test but let's be honest, she just didn't want to miss an after-school make-out session with Bobby.[15] So it was just Tiffany and me. Even Tiffany seemed like she was looking forward to the day with Mom and the only thing Tiffany looked forward to was prom.

I swear, my eyelids had just shut when our light switch flipped on and Mom called, "Rise and shine!" Really loudly.

Tiffany moaned and pulled her watch close to her eyeballs. "Five A.M.!"

I looked up at Mom to give her a piece of my mind, but then I noticed something terrible. Not only was she smiling, she was also dressed and ready to go. "You can't be serious, lady."

"Oh I am very serious. And don't call me *lady*."

~~~~~~~~~~~~~~~~~

15. And let's be double honest. The only French Layla knew was French kissing.

I brushed my teeth, changed into my clothes, wrapped my scarf around my neck, and combed my hair, or at least I thought that's what I was doing. I couldn't really tell because my eyes were still closed. I stumbled blindly into the kitchen and ran into someone I didn't expect. Layla. She was filling the coffeepot with water.

I opened one eye. "Are you sleepwalking?"

"I'm always up this early," she yawned.

"You are?"

"Yeah. How do you think Dad gets into his wheelchair every morning? Do you think he just magically appears there?"

Actually I did. In fact, sometimes I thought he was faking the whole thing.[16]

"But the sun isn't even up!"

She let out a big sigh. "I know."

While I poured a glass of juice Layla lined up all of Dad's pills on the counter and put the remote next to his table. I was just about to ask her how long she'd been getting up this early when Mom came in and kissed her on the cheek.

"Okay honey. Don't forget to put socks on Dad before you go. His feet get cold."

"Does Maggie need a lunch today?" Layla asked.

I almost choked on my orange juice. Was this why real fruit had replaced my fruit snacks?

---

16. He wasn't.

"*You've* been making my lunch?" I opened my other eye.

"No lunch for Maggie." Mom reached for the doorknob. "We're going to get something at the hotel."

Man, how long had this been going on? And more importantly, when would I get my fruit snacks back?

Mom hurried Tiffany and me into the car. I nudged Tiffany.

"Did you know Layla helps Dad in the morning?"

Tiffany mumbled, "I'm asleep."

"Did you know she makes my lunch too?"

"Yeah, she's been doing it since Mom started working. Get a clue. Now leave me alone. I need my beauty rest."

"You're going to need a lot more than half an hour," I said under my breath.

Mom drove while Tiffany and I yawned and fought the bags pulling down our eyes. As we cruised downtown, skyscrapers scraped the sky and headlights danced in the dark even though it was morning, not night. We inched our way closer and closer to the hotel until finally Mom exited the freeway and we went into a deep dark garage, down and down underneath the city above, and pulled into a parking spot between two Dumpsters. Gross. Tiffany and I clung to Mom's side as she led us to a bank of elevators between other Dumpsters that smelled like a cross between bad stuff and more bad stuff.

When the elevator doors opened, a rush of clean cold hit us and we walked into a lobby that looked like it belonged in a palace far, far away. Mom said she usually walked in through the loading dock but she wanted us to get the big deal picture of the big deal place where she worked. Tiffany and I couldn't stop looking. Up at the chandeliers dripping with what had to be real diamonds. Up at plants hanging from iron baskets. Down at Mom's back as she made a sudden stop and cleaned a scuff off the floor with her heel. I was just about to ask her why she was doing that when she waved us toward a door that was hidden behind a giant flowerpot. Awesome! SECRET PASSAGES!

We spiraled down a damp and dark staircase into a damp and dark hallway. Did this place have a dungeon? COOL. We passed bin after bin of dirty sheets, stained tablecloths, and towels kissed with lipstick. Tiffany held her nose to escape the smell of mildew and I pulled my scarf in front of my face just in case a goblin attacked me. We followed a loud rumble as the air got hotter and hotter. Oh. My. God. Maybe we were going to see a DRAGON![17] We turned the corner and I closed my eyes, too scared to see a mythical lizard. When I opened them, there was no giant creature, just row after row of giant washing machines and dryers. Where were we?

---

17. What? Dragons could technically exist. They're just like dinosaurs only they breathe fire. And fly. And live in medieval castles. Okay, well maybe they couldn't.

Mom scooted past a giant iron and giant gallons of detergent into a tiny room with no windows. She pulled open a cabinet door, put her purse inside, and locked it.

"Well, what do you think?"

What did I think? How about where in the h-e-double-hockey-sticks were we?!

I turned around and tried to take it all in. There were concrete floors and sea-foam-green walls. There were ancient filing cabinets and a box filled with tiny soaps and bottles. Tiffany pocketed a couple tiny lotions and I sat down in Mom's chair and started to spin. When I came to a stop, I saw a blur of my family in picture frames. There was Tiffany's dance team photo. Layla in a tutu and toe shoes. And me sleeping in a laundry basket complete with thumb in mouth. Embarrassing. I turned that picture around and picked up a seashell from a jar. I held it to my ear and listened for the ocean.

Mom picked up the one next to it. "This one sounds like South Carolina. It's from our trip last year. Remember?"

I nodded yes and reached for another.

"That's from the Outer Banks. And this one's from Savannah." She had an entire collection of shells and sand from all the beaches we'd visited. An entire coastline of memories in mason jars. I looked over at Tiffany, who was inspecting her nail polish for chips. Was she not wondering what I was wondering? Why did our mom work in this scary place?

"So when do we get to see famous people?" Tiffany asked. It was the smartest thing she'd ever said.

Mom grabbed a keychain with a billion keys on it from her desk drawer. "No famous people today. There's a teacher convention in town so we'll be dealing with them mostly."

"Teachers!" Tiffany looked disgusted. "The one day I get to skip school and I have to spend it with teachers! Gross!"

Even grosser? We weren't spending the day with teachers, we were spending the day cleaning their messes. I imagined it was going to be a lot of broken chalk and rotting apples.

We walked back into the laundry dungeon, where Mom dropped us off with a guy named Jesus. He wasn't the real Jesus and his name was pronounced "Hey Zeus," which I thought was funny because Zeus was a completely different god altogether. I didn't think he could turn water into wine but he did use water to get a wine stain out of a tablecloth and maybe it wasn't a miracle but it was impressive. He pushed a towel bin our way and pointed to a huge washing machine. "These go in there."

On towel five I was already exhausted.

"Excuse me, sir? How many of these do we have to put in there?"

Jesus laughed. "Oh, just about five hundred more."

"You've got to be kidding me?"

Jesus wasn't kidding.

I proposed a plan. "I vote we give up."

"No way. Mom will just give us more to do."

"You're right."

Tiffany looked surprised.

"I know. It sounded weird when I said it."

We pulled up our bootstraps and did our best even though I felt like my arms were going to fall off. When Mom finally returned and said it was time to go upstairs, we reeked of Tide and sweat. Phew. I was glad that was over.

Mom took us up a secret elevator and through a secret door to a room called the presidential suite, but there was nothing presidential about it. No Oval Office. No tour with tourists. No Secret Service. Mom said really rich people stayed there and from what I could see these people were slobs with a capital SLOBS.

Tiffany and I rolled up our cardigan sleeves and gathered all of the giant sheets from the giant bed, while Mom piled dishes on top of one another.

"You do this every day?" Tiffany asked.

"Every single day," Mom said.

Tiffany washed windows and I collected all of the towels from the bathroom floor. One had a stain that looked like two bats and I threw it back on the floor praying I hadn't caught flesh-eating bacteria.

"Can we please stop?" Tiffany begged. "I have broken like thirty nails."

I rolled my eyes. "You only have twenty nails."

Mom checked her watch. "Well, it *is* lunchtime."

Yes! I loved lunchtime.

We breezed into the hotel restaurant, where prime rib sizzled and banana pudding was piled in heaps. Even the vegetables looked good. I reached for a plate from a giant stack and plotted my plan of attack. But suddenly my mission was diverted when Mom put the plate back on the stack.

"This food is for guests, Maggie. We're going to the cafeteria."

Cafeteria! What kind of sick joke was this?

We passed through another secret door into a big scary room that smelled like mashed potatoes and Windex. Mom told us to get whatever we wanted, which for the very first time did not sound appetizing. I found a box of cereal and carton of milk that looked safe and Tiffany grabbed a bruised banana and the only granola bar not covered in chocolate because she thinks chocolate gives you zits even though I knew that was just a myth.[18]

We sat next to a gaggle of ladies lost in a blur of Spanish. Mom chatted with them in Spanglish that I didn't even know she knew. I concentrated on my cereal, not wanting them to know they lost me at *"hola,"* which wasn't my fault. I blamed the public school system. Anyway, one lady named Maria pointed at Tiffany and cooed, *"Muy bonita,"* which made Tiffany smile her

~~~~~~~~~~~~~~~

18. Hey Zeus, please let it be a myth.

toothy beauty queen smile. Another lady mumbled something to me but before I could muster a "*Qué?*" my mom interrupted, "Well, she looks just like her father." Man, where was Jesus when you needed him? Probably still downstairs folding towels.

After lunch, we went back to the lobby to check on the giant plants in the giant baskets. As Mom snapped a yellow leaf off a vine, a tall guy in a fancy suit and shiny shoes tapped her on the shoulder. Finally! A famous person! Who was this guy? Maybe a president or an Olympian or one of those TV priests?

Mom straightened her jacket and greeted him. "Oh, hi Mr. Grant. Girls, this is Mr. Grant. My boss." Okay, not famous. But he was still kind of a big deal, so I curtsied.[19]

Mr. Grant took my hand and shook my whole body. "You know, your mother is a real go-getter, girls. She's one of our best. She'll make her way to supervisor in no time. She really keeps this place running like a well-oiled machine."

She did? What did she know about machines? This was the same lady who when the hot water stopped working in the bathroom said to just use cold water. And when we protested she told us cold water was way better for our complexions, which Layla and Tiffany believed but I didn't because I'm not an idiot. How did she do so much? And then, I figured it out.

---

19. I don't know why I curtsied.

Mom was a mom to all of these people. And being a mom is what Mom did best.

She made all their beds and cleaned all their dishes and made sure all of their days and nights were tidy and perfect.

No wonder she was tired all the time and kept sea-shells at her desk. She probably just wanted to be reminded that somewhere there was sand she could sink her toes into. Somewhere out there she wouldn't have to clean scuffs off a marble floor, couldn't catch flesh-eating bacteria from a towel.

On the car ride home, I fought sleep with thoughts of everything Mom did without exploding. I mean, spontaneous combustion is a real thing because it's in the dictionary. How did she do so much? And then I had a thought: Maybe she was powered by all of her freckles.

Mom was covered in freckles from head to toe. Maybe each one gave her energy to do every single thing she had to do. Maybe each one was a dish done, a towel folded, a dinner made. Maybe the ones clustered by her heart were for Layla, Dad, and me, and maybe even Tiffany. Maybe every cluster was like a constellation that powered her through one big deal to the next.

As we walked inside, I grabbed Mom's hand. I was going to tell her thank you. I was going to tell her I loved her. But I didn't. Because when we walked in the door, Dad was lying on the floor.

CHAPTER FIVE

My heart leapt into my throat and Layla leapt from beside Dad and ran into Mom's arms.

"Thank God you're home! I tried to pick him up but I couldn't and I didn't know what to do. I got him to sit up but I couldn't carry him. I wanted to call 911 but Dad wouldn't let me and I just—"

Layla was talking so fast and she sounded so scared. Mom squeezed her close to her side and turned to Dad.

"Danny, are you okay?"

Her voice sounded weird and shaky but Dad's voice sounded just like Dad.

"Better than ever," he smiled. "Go ahead, I got this."

Mom stepped around Dad and walked down the hall with Layla pulled so close they almost looked like one person. "Girls, help your dad okay? I'll be right back."

Where was she going?! We had a major situation and she was worried about Layla?! Layla wasn't lying on the floor! Layla's legs were wide awake!

I ran to the phone and hit 9 immediately. I'd always wanted to call 911. It had always seemed so thrilling when Smokey Bear talked about it. So high-stakes. So heroic. But right then it just felt necessary.

Tiffany yanked the phone out of my hands before I got to the 1-1.

"What are you doing?!"

"I'm calling for help! What do you think I'm doing?!"

She put the phone back on the receiver. "He's on the floor. Not on fire. Now, grab an arm and a leg. We're going to pick him up."

"We can't pick him up! He probably weighs four hundred pounds!"

Dad didn't like that. "Excuse me! I am a very solid one-sixty. Have been since I was seventeen. Now who wants to get Twister from the closet? I've been warming up for hours."

Tiffany giggled. "No way. You couldn't beat me."

"I beat Layla. Why do you think she's so upset?" Dad winked.

"Because you're on the floor!" I yelled.

"Am I?" he joked. "I hadn't noticed."

Tiffany put her arms around Dad's chest. "Maggie, grab an arm and a leg."

I did what she said which felt weird because I never did what she said.

"We're going to pick him up on the count of three, okay?"

I was nervous. Dad's ice-cold arms and legs pressed against mine.

"Ready? One . . . two . . ."

"No! Stop!" I yelled. "We should wait for Mom. I'll drop him."

This was one of those times Mom would have wanted me to pull up my bootstraps. But I just couldn't and Dad agreed with me.

"Yeah, let's just wait. I don't want to get dropped. I fell off the stage at a Stones concert once and I don't want to relive that again."

"You can do it, Maggie," Tiffany insisted. "Just use your knees and not your back. Ready?"

For some reason I believed her. I pulled my meta-phorical bootstraps as close to my knees as they would get. And when I heard three, we stood together and carried Dad back into his chair.

Tiffany gave me a little shove. "Good job, Maggie."

I held my aching back like an old lady. "Thanks."

Dad tugged his sleepy arm with his less sleepy arm back onto his armrests. "Thank you, girls. I promise to not do that again."

I stood back and surveyed the damage. Dad's table was toppled over on the floor. His pills were scattered everywhere and the TV remote was in pieces next to his ashtray. Cigarette butts were flung all over the carpet and ash covered everything, including the *National Geographic* about Pompeii, which was funny, but not at the time.

I kneeled down and picked up a handful of pills. "What happened, Dad?"

"Oh, it was just an accident. I dropped a cigarette on the floor and when I went to pick it up, I lost my balance and fell out of the chair. It's no big deal."

It certainly seemed like a big deal. It seemed like a big deal deep down in my guts and it seemed like a big deal because Layla was crying and it seemed like a big deal because Mom was with her and it seemed like a big deal because I had never picked Dad up before. That was Mom's job.

Tiffany kneeled next to me and put the remote back together. "Go get Dad a blanket," she whispered.

"Why?" I whispered back even though I didn't know why we were whispering.

"He looks cold."

I remembered his ice-cold arms and legs and I stood up and headed down the hall. I opened the closet just as Mom was closing Layla's door.

"Hey, sweetheart. What do you need?"

Mom's eyes were fuzzy and the freckles on her face were flushed with red.

"Um, I'm getting a blanket for Dad. Is everything okay?

Is Layla okay?" I reached for her door. "Maybe I can help?"

"Don't worry. Everybody's fine. Layla's just tired. Let's leave her alone to rest, okay? How's Dad?"

"I picked him up. Well, Tiffany and I picked him up, but I did most of the lifting. I'm a lot stronger than I look."

Mom smiled. "Yes, you are."

I got a blanket for Dad and we went back to the living room, where Tiffany was brushing his hair.

"Look at me, I'm as good as new!"

Mom kissed Dad's cheek. "Decided to take up yoga, I assume?"

Tiffany laughed. "No, Twister."

Everyone was joking and laughing and gallivanting but I had to get down to business. "Dad! YOU HAVE TO STOP SMOKING! You could have burned the house down!"

Tiffany agreed. "Seriously Dad, it's really uncool."

"Come on," he said. "It makes me look kind of cool."

Dad was sort of obsessed with being cool. In fact, before his legs fell asleep he did all kinds of supercool stuff like cartwheels and somersaults. I don't remember any of it, but Layla does. One time, she even saw Dad do a backflip. This was when his balance was just getting fuzzy. And Layla held his cane and Mom held his hand and when he let go, he did a full rotation in the air before landing on his feet. He toppled over a second later, but he nailed the landing. He. Nailed. The. Landing. Layla said he didn't stop smiling for a week and sometimes even now he'll say, "Remember the backflip, Layla Hayla?"[20] And Layla will roll her eyes and say, "Yeah Dad, I remember. You nailed the landing."

But he had to give up whatever cool he thought smoking gave him and Tiffany wouldn't let it go until he was convinced. "I'm your coolest daughter, Dad, and I swear there is nothing cool about smoking."

"Okay, okay," Dad said. "I hear you."

Layla came into the living room. "What's going on?"

"We're forcing Dad to give up smoking for the greater good of our lungs and humanity," I explained.

Layla nodded. "It really is disgusting, Dad."

"Okay, okay. I'll quit. I promise." Dad looked up at Layla with a smile. "Just for you."

While Dad was a-okay, something was still bothering me. I had never thought about Dad being alone with his legs fast asleep and what that meant. It had never seemed dangerous—until tonight when we found him on the floor. His hands and feet were getting more and more sleepy. And I wished I knew why.

~~~~~~~~~~~~

20. When Layla was little Dad called her "Layla Hayla" because he thought she was the bee's knees. He calls me "Mags" because it sounds cool and he calls Tiffany "Tiffany" because if you call her anything else, she loses her mind.

Maybe I could figure out how to wake them up? Every time I tried to look up his disease though, my resources were lacking. For some reason, we never had an M encyclopedia and the one thing I knew about his disease was that the first word started with an *m*. So not only did I know nothing about it, I also didn't know anything about mammoths, the Milky Way, or Montana.

Mom never let me read the pamphlets while we waited for Dad at the doctor's office either. She'd say they were filled with propaganda and then I'd say, "Geez hippie, calm down." And then she'd take my M&M's away and then I'd say I was sorry and then she'd give me the M&M's back and then we'd take quizzes in magazines to find out if we were summers or falls.[21]

I'd have to step up my research about the sleepiness. Right after I stepped up my research about the migration of monarch butterflies for my science project, but before I stepped up my research about Franklin Roosevelt and his sleepy legs. It only seemed right to figure out Dad's sleeping legs first.

I went to the bathroom to give my face a good splash of cold water, hoping it would scare away any residual weirdness I had left inside. When I pulled the towel away from my face, Mom was next to me.

"So everyone's voted for pizza for dinner. You in?"

"Sounds good." I shrugged.

~~~~~~~~~~~~

21. I'm a fall.

"You don't sound too excited for pizza. And you're always excited for pizza."

"I don't know." I couldn't find the right words. I felt like there was so much to say and also nothing to say at all. But I tried. "That was scary."

"Oh Maggie, Dad's fine. You saw him. He's totally fine."

"Then why do I feel so weird? Should we be scared?"

Mom knelt in front of me.

"We shouldn't be scared, honey. Not even a little."

She took my hand and squeezed.

"We should be brave."

CHAPTER SIX

Dad's fall led to more fall but of the autumn variety. The leaves turned and the temperature dropped and some other stuff happened that wasn't really important because then it was Halloween. Halloween! The single best day of the year! The day I would make a national holiday once I was president. Schools would be closed but banks would stay open and instead of money they would hand out buckets and buckets of candy!

Layla and Tiffany were both home on Halloween night, which was weird because they should've been at parties dressed up as hotter versions of themselves. But Halloween was on a school night and Mom never allows hotness on school nights. So they stayed in and helped me get ready for trick-or-treating.[22] They tried

---

22. What? I'm still a kid. I can trick-or-treat. There's nothing wrong with it.

to convince me to be a ton of things involving makeup, high heels, and tight dresses but I opted for an homage to one of my heroes: Albert Einstein.

Layla teased my hair into a tizzy and Tiffany sprayed it white with Halloween hair dye. We used Dad as a model for my mustache and Layla penciled in the perfect whiskers with eyeliner. I made a bow tie out of my scarf, put on a sweater, and ta-da! I was a genius.

I was so excited to hit the streets, but for some reason Dad wasn't feeling great. Probably because I told him I wouldn't share any candy with him, which was only 90% true because I'd give him all my Smarties because I hated Smarties because they are like fake candy. Anyway. I begged him to go with me because he'd never been with me and Mom was stuck at work and kids who trick-or-treat alone get kidnapped.

"Okay, I'll go, but I don't have a costume."

That's when I had the best idea ever. I found a stack of black and gray construction paper and started cutting. I cut out a few big boulders and Scotch Taped them to his shirt. "Ta-da! Let's hit the streets."

"Wait, what am I?"

I tapped the wheel on his chair. "You're the Rolling Stones!"

"Ha, that's pretty cool." He laughed and we rolled out the door.

Layla and Tiffany joined us halfway up the driveway in their last-minute costumes. Layla wore a sweatshirt with the neck cut out and said she was an aerobics instructor and Tiffany wore a sweatshirt with the neck cut out and said she was a punk rocker. Whatever. All that mattered was they were there and we were together and they could take over pushing Dad up the hill because my arms were about to break off.

We knocked on all kinds of doors and every time I explained Dad's costume I got a big laugh and an extra handful of candy, which made me think, I should bring this guy everywhere.

On our way down the hill, Layla and Tiffany headed back home early because they had eaten too much candy and by too much I mean three candy corn. I was sharing a Twix with Dad when I heard someone shout my name. And that someone was an angel sent straight from heaven. Even though he was dressed as a zombie sent from that other place. It was Clyde.

My knees buckled as Clyde walked his bike over to Dad and me.

"I thought that was you. You look great! Albert Einstein, right?"

God, we had so much in common. I also thought I looked great.

"Yeah, Albert Einstein. I love him. Well not like that. I don't LOVE him. We'd just be friends if he were alive. Nothing more. So, what are you? A zombie?"

Dad answered before Clyde could. "You're a zombie Buddy Holly. Right?"

Clyde's face lit up. "You're the only one who's gotten my costume all night!"

"Really? The black glasses make you a dead ringer." Dad nudged me. "Get it? *Dead* ringer?"

I wanted to disappear. I couldn't believe that Dad would humiliate me at this critical moment in my relationship with Clyde. But Clyde laughed so I just laughed too.

"I tried to get my brother to be the Big Bopper. But he wanted to be James Bond."

"Sean Connery James Bond right?" Dad asked.

Clyde smiled. "Yeah."

"Because he had the coolest cars."

Clyde nodded. "Exactly. Well, I better go. My mom will kill me if I'm late for dinner."

"That's impossible," I pointed out. "You're already dead."

"I guess you're right." Clyde laughed. "But I don't want to chance it."

He got on his bike. "It was nice meeting you, Mr. Mayfield. See you at school, Maggie." And then he rode away into the moonlight.

Dad unlocked his wheels and turned toward me. "So that's Clyde?"

"That's Clyde," I sighed with my whole heart in my throat.

"You're right. He is really cool. And he thinks you look great."

"I know!"

When we got home, Mom already had dinner ready and I pulled on my PJs but left my hair crazy because it was hilarious. Dad wheeled himself over to the stereo and put on *Sticky Fingers* by the Rolling Stones and the house lit up with "Brown Sugar." We took our seats and I blessed the Lord for these our gifts of spaghetti and meatballs. And then Dad dropped his fork.

No big deal, right? His fingers were probably still sticky from the Snickers we snuck before dinner.[23] He picked his fork up again, guided it to his noodles, lifted it to his mouth—and dropped it all over his Cream T-shirt. Now Eric Clapton was eating Dad's spaghetti.

His next attempt was more determined, more focused. He gripped the handle of the fork with his whole hand,[24] scooped, and lifted again. The whole bite dropped into his lap.

Layla and Tiffany locked eyes with their plates while I sank into my scarf. I don't know why. I just felt weird.

Dad took a deep breath. "No one eats until I can."

Really? Really. This was serious. The house was silent except for the murmur of Mick Jagger singing about

---

23. In fact maybe the Rolling Stones were in a similar predicament when they named the album.

24. Holding a fork like this is totally against the Law of Mom but it felt wrong to call him out on it right then.

wild horses. A million butterflies took off in my stomach. We put our forks to sleep on beds of asparagus and watched as Dad tried again. But this time when he dropped the fork, he dropped his head to his chest too.

Mom sprang up. "Let's get some fresh air, okay?" She wheeled Dad out into the garage. Layla, Tiffany, and I kept our eyes down and we waited. We waited and waited and waited.

On minute ten of waiting, I picked up my fork and went for a bite.

Layla threw her napkin at me. "Stop it. You heard Dad."

My stomach growled like it was sticking up for me. "But I'm starving." Emphasis on *starving*.

Tiffany grabbed my fork from my hand. "How can you be starving? I saw you scarf that Snickers before dinner."

I grabbed my fork back. "It was a mini Snickers! And Mom would want us to eat. What's the big deal anyway? I drop my fork all the time."

"It's a huge deal!" Tiffany yelled.

"Why?"

Before Tiffany could let me have it, Layla interrupted. "Stop it, Tiffany."

Hold on, people. Did everyone know something I didn't? "What's going on?"

Before they could answer, the door opened and Mom rolled Dad back inside. Their eyes were red and Dad had a smear of lipstick on his cheek. Mom stacked the still-full plates on top of each other and sighed.

"Who wants ice cream for dinner?"

I had no idea what was going on, but I did know one thing. I definitely wanted ice cream for dinner.

Mom scooped chocolate almond ice cream into mugs and passed them around the table. She took a bite from her cup and spooned a scoop into Dad's mouth while the record needle softly skipped reminding us that there was a second side to *Sticky Fingers* that needed to be heard.

I stirred my ice cream into a milkshake, drank it down, and let myself slip into a sugar coma trying to forget the fork, the weird, and the butterflies.

The next day I swore I'd get to the bottom of whatever it was that everyone else knew and I didn't. But when I woke up, I had mustache on my neck, cheeks, and eyelids and it took a while to scrub off. And then I had to get to school and I couldn't think about it there because I only think about school at school because there's just so much to think about at school. And then when I got home, I was preoccupied with my trick-or-treating loot. Inspecting every single piece for poison took time and precision. But when I finally finished, I decided to take Dad a boatload of unpoisonous Smarties.

I tiptoed into the living room because I felt like we should still be tiptoeing both literally and metaphorically. The night before still rumbled weird in my belly. Well, it could have been the SweeTarts rumbling weird in there but I was pretty sure it was just residual weird from what happened at dinner. So I decided it might be best if my mission to deliver the Smarties to Dad was as covert as possible. I walked up behind his chair so he couldn't see me and slowly stacked them on his table, then started moonwalking back to my room.

"Hey, Albert!"

Busted.

"Why don't you unroll me a couple sleeves?"

I gave up my cover and turned back. "It's just Maggie. Albert is nevermore."

"Wouldn't that be Edgar?[25]" Dad winked.

I piled a bunch of Smarties onto a napkin and ate one.[26]

"Maybe I'll be Edgar Allan Poe next year." Suddenly I was really excited. "Wanna be my raven?"

His face lit up but only dimly. "Hmmm, maybe."

Whatever. I turned to leave but he called me back.

"Hey Mags, check out this whopper."

---

25. Sometimes I forget how smart Dad is. Probably because he always promotes himself as good looking first, brilliant second.

26. Nope, still tasted fake.

"What? Did you steal my Whoppers?!"[27]

"No, geez. I'm talking about the bruise on my foot." I looked down. A light purple bruise covered his entire foot. It was impressive as far as bruises go and I knew a lot about bruises. I was covered in them.

"That's nothing. Look at this one on my arm." I rolled up my sleeve and presented a black orb above my elbow. I looked back at his foot. "How'd you get it?"

"Dropped the shaving cream. What about you?"

"Ran into the pantry door."

He cracked up. "But the pantry's always in the same place."

"I dunno . . . it just snuck up on me."

He was seeming more and more like my cool dude dad from before. More like my cool dude dad who would tell me anything.

"Hey Dad. Is, um, everything okay?"

"Hmm. Is everything okay?"

He rolled the Smarties back and forth on the table and then threw three in his mouth.

"Well, one huge thing happened last night. One huge thing that changes everything."

He paused and I held my breath.

"Last night Clyde realized you're the coolest girl that ever was."

----

27. The candy that rivals any other in originality, crunch, and overall deliciousness.

I blushed and smiled and gathered up every last wrapper to throw away in the trash outside so Mom wouldn't know I had exceeded her two-pieces-of-candy-a-day limit by ten pieces. The rumbling weird in my belly was replaced by a rumbling ache but it wasn't because I was scared. It was just because I ate five Whoppers. And a Crunch bar. And maybe a candy corn or three. It definitely wasn't because I was scared.

CHAPTER SEVEN

A few weeks later Dad was back to his old Dad self. He even tried to get me to watch a scary movie, but I refused. "Mom says I'm not allowed to watch that kind of stuff."

"We don't have to tell Mom," he whispered.

"No way, José," I whispered back.

We were flipping through the channels and looking for something unterrifying when something so scary happened I almost died. And it wasn't on TV. It was right next to us.

Tiffany cruised by us wearing something super tight and super short and her face looked like she was competing in some kind of makeup Olympics where instead of medals they handed out fake eyelashes. The scariest part? She grabbed the car keys and walked right out the door.

Dad nudged me. "Oooh. Wanna watch *Wild America*? I love Marty Stouffer."

"Dad! You can't let Tiffany leave! She's not allowed to be hot on school nights!"

"Oh, I didn't know that. What should I do?"

"Go after her!"

He wheeled over to the door and looked out the window. "Too late. She's already gone. Maybe she'll be right back?"

"Dressed like that? No way. I bet she's halfway to Vegas by now."

"Don't you think you're overreacting?"

I shook my head. "She broke one of Mom's biggest rules!"

"Your mom has so many rules. How am I supposed to remember all of them?"

That's when I dashed into my [28] bedroom and pulled my third most important notebook out from under my bed. I went back to the living room and flipped right to page five. "See, it's rule number twenty-seven. No hotness on school nights."

Dad stared. "What is this?"

"It's my Law of Mom book. I wrote down every single one of her rules."

He was speechless as he paged through page after page of rule after rule, which I expected since sometimes

---

28. Well it was 50% my bedroom. More like 30% when Tiffany was going through a break-up. Closer to 20% when she was grounded.[1]

    1. Which was 90% of the time.

I even blew my own mind. I pointed out one of my favorites: "No peanut butter knife in the jelly jar." Honestly, it's just common courtesy.

"Does your mother know about this?" he said at last.

"Oh yeah, she helped me write it just before she went to work."

Dad nodded. "Of course she did."

The next day I knew something was wrong on my walk home from the bus stop. At first, I thought I'd forgotten something at school. So I stopped mid-driveway and went through my book bag, which was packed to the brim since we were now on Thanksgiving break and I wanted to keep up with my studies between slices of pie. Math notebook? Check. English notebook? Check. History paper with a big red A on it? Check. French dictionary? Check in French. Personal copy of *The Secret Garden* with my personal notes? Check. School copy of *The Secret Garden* with my school notes? Check. Empty bag of candy corn? Check. Nothing was missing. Nothing was out of order. And there was a rogue candy corn at the bottom of my bag, so that was good.

But I still had that sick-to-my-stomach feeling. That's when I got worried that something had happened to Dad. What if he'd fallen again? I picked up my pace to a fast walk and swung open the front door. But it wasn't Dad who was in trouble. It was Tiffany.

Picture it. Tiffany Mayfield, who's already a web of long arms and long legs, tangled with another set of long arms and long legs belonging to a boy. A BOY! On the couch. ON THE COUCH!

Before secretly reading an uncomfortable essay in Layla's *Seventeen* magazine a month before, I would've thought this was s-e-x on the c-o-u-c-h. But now I knew that it wasn't. They were just wrapped in a sleep hug. But it was still bad, bad, bad. And there next to the couch was our dad and he was mad, mad, mad.

Dad was red-faced and yelling at Tiffany and the boy to GET UP. But they didn't budge because popular teenagers sleep in a near comatose state because their brains are filled with nothing. Tiffany was probably dreaming about dance team nothingness and the boy was probably dreaming about football nothingness and it is hard to yell teenagers out of this deep nothing sleep.

So I shook them. I yanked Tiffany's arm. "Tiffany, WAKE UP! WAKE UP!"

Tiffany yawned. "What?"

The boy pulled her tighter and now Dad was even more furious. If there was ever a time for a miracle to wake his legs up, IT WAS RIGHT NOW.

Dad screamed, "GET OUT! GET OUT NOW!" This time the boy heard him and he jumped up, ran out the door, and peeled out of the driveway.

Tiffany picked up the blankets and sauntered down the hall. "God Dad, calm down. We were just sleeping."

"Come back here, young lady!"

Tiffany kept walking.

Uh-oh.

"I'm serious, Tiffany!"

She went into our room and slammed the door.

Oh no, she didn't.

OH YES. SHE. DID.

I didn't think Dad was freaking out enough, so I unlocked his wheels and pushed him down the hall. "You can't let her get away with this, Dad!"

He waved my hand away from his chair. "Stop it, Maggie."

"Mom would go after her!"

He held his wheels. "Mom's not here. Now push me back to the living room."

"But Dad . . ."

"NOW, Maggie."

I wheeled him back and for a long time, we sat in silence. I didn't get it. Why weren't we yelling? Why weren't we handing out serious punishment? Why weren't we calling Mom?

"What are we doing, Dad?"

He kept a steely focus on the hallway. "We're fighting a war of attrition."

Cool! We were wearing down the enemy by trapping her in a room with no phone, no food, no access to the outside world. Man, Dad was so smart. He knew that eventually, even a fox has to come out of its hole. To arm our defense even further, Dad showed me the ransom he was holding in his chair: Tiffany's makeup bag. Ha. Amazing. She wasn't going anywhere. Tiffany hadn't left the house without makeup since birth.

After an hour passed I had my doubts, but on hour two, his plan worked. The door creaked open, and quiet long-legged footsteps tiptoed down the hall. When Tiffany turned the corner, she found Dad and me with our arms crossed, waiting for her.

Dad spoke first. "Well hello, Tiffany."

I echoed him like a corporal to a captain. "Well hello, Tiffany."

"Okay, Maggie. You can go to your room now."

"No way, Dad. We're in this together."

"Go. Now."

Fine. FINE. I walked to my room and pretended to shut the door. When the coast was clear, I snuck back and hid behind the couch. No way was I going to miss this. This was going to be good and I needed to hear every detail. It wasn't every day that Law of Mom rule forty-five[29] was broken.

"I don't know what the big deal is, Dad," Tiffany huffed. "We were just sleeping." What an idiot defense.

~~~~~~~~~~~~~

29. No boys allowed in the house.

Dad let out a deep breath. "There's no way you're spooning[30] with boys on my couch under my roof." Well played, Dad. Well. Played.

"It's not fair. Layla's boyfriend is over all the time and you never yell at her. She's your favorite!"

Amazing. Not only was this a good argument, it was totally true. In Dad's eyes, Layla could do no wrong. When Layla came home from spring break with blond hair, Mom freaked but Dad just sighed, "Well, blondes do have more fun." When Layla failed geometry, it was the teacher's fault. When Layla needed money, he always opened his wallet. But when Tiffany wanted money he always asked, "What for?" And when I wanted money, he always said, "No more candy, Maggie." Layla was the favorite and we all knew it.

"This isn't about Layla. It's about you."

Tiffany burst into tears. I almost felt bad for her. I put myself in her shoes.[31] I thought about Clyde and me on that couch. Hugging our guts out while watching a documentary about whales because we're thoughtful and adorable. I thought about our mansion and our Porsche and the 2.5 kids we would have according to the last

---

30. I hoped he wasn't banning all spooning because I ate some serious ice cream on that couch.

31. Even though I would never wear her shoes because they were too tall and I liked to be down low where the action was.

game of MASH I played. And then I had a mini panic attack and reminded myself, "Career first, Maggie. Love second."

Dad wheeled over to Tiffany and tried to console her. "I'm just worried about you, honey. I see so much of myself in you, which is good because I'm really cool, but bad because I've done some really uncool things. I don't want you to make the same mistakes I made."

Whoa, that was heavy and Dad never got heavy. Where had it come from? I racked my brain. Was it a Dylan lyric? Maybe an early Springsteen rarity? I couldn't come up with anything. I decided it must have been a Dad original.

Tiffany was too Tiffany to understand what he meant so she unleashed the line she'd fed Mom many times before. "I just want you to love me for me, Dad."

Dad wasn't buying it. "You can't use that on me. I invented that in, like, 1968."

Tiffany sobbed some more and I think Dad was getting sick of it because he changed the subject entirely. "Did I ever tell you about Patty Applegate?"

"N-n-n-n-no."

Dad time traveled and this time he went back to when he was Tiffany's age. Apparently, Patty Applegate was the head cheerleader when Dad was on the football team. It was the beginning of his senior year and he had a real shot at quarterback. But then he started seeing Patty and got distracted and by the first game, he'd missed too many practices to even be considered for quarterback. And the worst part? Patty dumped him a week later for the kid who did make quarterback.

"And that guy wasn't even half as good looking as me," Dad said. I wasn't really sure what kind of lesson he was trying to teach here but Tiffany seemed to get it. And Tiffany doesn't get anything. She can barely work the hair dryer.

Tiffany promised no more boys in the house and Dad promised no more embarrassing freak-outs.

"Okay, Maggie. You can come out now."

Busted. I tried to cover my tracks. "Oh hey. I lost a pen. Thought it might be under here."

Tiffany gave me the evil eye. "Oh, really. Did you find it?"

"No, I didn't. But I did find a boy back here. Is he yours?"

Tiffany looked like she might murder me.

Dad held up his hand. "That's enough, Maggie."

Just as Tiffany and I were about to get into it BIG TIME, headlights flashed across the wall. Yes! Mom was home! I headed for the door, but Dad cut me off.

"I'll tell her what happened, Maggie. Why don't you just go start on your homework?"

"I don't have any homework. I did it all on the bus. Can't I greet my hard-working mother at the door because I love her?"

"No."

He was on to me. So I sidestepped his chair.

"AND I need to tell Mom something really importa—"

He stopped me again. "I'll get the door. You go do something else. Something useful." Whatever.

I waited for Dad to open the door but when he did, Mom wasn't even there. It was Layla! And she was mid-lip-lock with her boyfriend, Bobby. Ha! Amazing!

Layla finally came up for air. "Oh hi, Daddy. I was just coming in."

Bobby wiped Layla's lip gloss off his mouth. "Hi, Mr. Mayfield. It sure is good to see you aga—"

Dad yanked Layla inside and slammed the door.

Layla lost it. "Daddy! What are you doing?"

"Go to your room! Everyone go to their rooms!"

Tiffany refused to go to our room if I was in there and Layla had to get something out of Bobby's truck and I desperately needed a juice box. Everyone was screaming when Mom opened the door.

"Hello? I'm home! What's going on in here?"

Dad yelled, "Everyone stop!" And then he made Mom push him into the garage.[32] I imagined what happened next was Dad filling Mom in on what terrible people Tiffany and Layla were turning out to be. And he probably told her I was the only daughter with any common sense and they should send me to a really fancy college

---

32. They talked in the garage more and more. I guess it was neutral territory. Kind of like Switzerland but with no Swiss Miss.

because I never ever disappointed them. But when Mom wheeled Dad back in, I got sent to my room and this time I actually went because Mom walked me there. Where was the trust?

Layla and Tiffany stayed in the living room and I heard a lot of mumbling followed by what I assumed was "Yes ma'am" and "Yes sir." When Mom opened my door, she almost knocked me and my ear out.

"Okay, Maggie. It's your turn."

Wait, was I getting in trouble?

I sulked into the living room and sat on the couch with my back turned away from the enemies who said they were my parents. I mean how could I know for sure if they were my real parents? I didn't have any concrete proof they weren't Russian spies. So what if they couldn't speak Russian. Maybe they were THAT good.

Mom made me turn around. "Maggie, we know that you have a lot of opinions. But when it comes to parenting, you have to leave it to me and your dad."

"I didn't do ANYTHING."

Dad shook his head. "Listen, Mags. You have to trust that I'm doing the right thing. You chiming in only makes matters worse."

Trust him! You had to be kidding me. I liked the guy, sure, but trusting him was questionable. He'd tricked me too many times. Like my first bike ride without training wheels. He SWORE he was right behind me and he wouldn't let go of the seat. And sure, I should've questioned how a guy with a cane was running. But still, he said that he was and I believed him. And then I fell and I cried and he said he was sorry but sorry didn't cut the ketchup.[33] So let's just say his track record with trust was spotty at best.

I wanted out of the living room so I promised to mind my own beeswax. But my fingers were crossed in my mind, so the promise didn't count.

We all went to bed kind of angry, even Layla, and she usually smiled so much it was annoying. But when I went to brush my teeth, she closed the bathroom door in my face. And she was never mad at me, mostly because she barely knew I was alive.

I crawled into bed, closed my eyes, and couldn't stop thinking about how my sisters just didn't get it. Boys were stupid. Well, all boys except for Clyde. And then I couldn't stop thinking about the good old days when Mom was always around. She maintained a certain level of order that I not only followed to a T, but respected to a T too. And so did Layla and Tiffany. Sure, getting to know Dad more was great and all but I always figured I would get to know him eventually. Like when he moved into the White House when I was president and I put him in charge of the rock 'n' roll archives at the Smithsonian.

I just wanted to go back. Back to how it used to be.

~~~~~~~~~~~~~~~

33. I hate mustard.

CHAPTER EIGHT

The next morning, Mom woke me up extra early to go get the last-minute staples for our Thanksgiving feast. We had to beat the crowd to the store and I was happy to spend some quality time with her. Plus, someone had to make sure we got extra jumbo marshmallows for the sweet potatoes and not just the regular jumbo kind. I got a cart and Mom navigated the store fearlessly. She's the Magellan[34] of grocery stores. We found everything we needed in less than ten minutes, checked out, and loaded the overflowing bags into the back of the car.

When my seat belt was buckled, I decided it was safe to get something really important off my chest. "So what's up with you and Dad?"

---

34. Magellan was an explorer. Kind of like Christopher Columbus. But with a way cool beard.

Mom looked overwhelmed. I could tell she was running through a number of possibilities in her mind but finally she just asked, "What do you mean?"

"I mean, why did you guys totally freak yesterday?"

"What are you talking about?"

I opened the marshmallow bag, put one in my mouth, and mumbled, "Evewyone has wost it. Waywa and Tiffany have wost it too."

Mom turned down the radio and pulled the bag out of my hands. "You girls have to understand that all of this change is hard for me too. And it's especially hard for your dad. All those years, you all were growing up while he was at work. He missed a lot. And now, he's home and there's a bunch of teenagers roaming around the place. And they are kissing boys and misbehaving." She looked at me when she said "misbehaving."

"I DIDN'T DO ANYTHING." I yelled it just one last time so she knew. For sure. That I had not. Done. ANYTHING.

She continued as if she hadn't heard me. "But to him, you all are still little girls."

I ate the last marshmallow I'd hidden in my pocket.

"Hey, I'm not a wittwe giw. I'm too smawt to be a wittwe giw."

"You know what I mean." She sighed.

When we pulled into the driveway, we could hear the speakers blasting inside the house. Dad had the stereo cranked up and playing *Bruce Springsteen Live* while Layla and Tiffany cleaned. I thought they would've been sulking through their punishment of getting the house ready for Thanksgiving, but they seemed to be enjoying themselves. Tiffany sang "Born to Run" into a roll of paper towels while Layla danced with the mop. I was happy to see she was just regular dancing with the mop, not dirty dancing. It would have been a shame to have to tell on her so close to Thanksgiving.

After everything was spotless and all the groceries were away, Mom started prepping for the next day's feast. Usually, she slaved away in the kitchen alone, while we did a bunch of nothing. But as Mom opened a bag of pecans, Tiffany asked, "Need any help?"

"Really?" Mom asked.

"I can make the pies."

I didn't know why Tiffany helped. Maybe she felt bad for almost giving Dad a heart attack the day before. Or maybe she was just bored watching *Spaceballs* with Dad and me for the billionth time although I don't know how that is possible because it is HILARIOUS. But either way, she helped Mom make the pumpkin, pecan, and chocolate pies and she even let me lick the spatulas. It was almost like we really liked each other. Almost.

The next day, we feasted! Halfway through the first course, Dad had an idea. "How about we each say what we're thankful for?"

Ugh, really Dad? Layla, Tiffany, and I rolled our eyes, but Dad insisted.

"I'm serious. Layla, you go first."

Layla cleared her throat. "I'm thankful for my car. Because it is badass."

Tiffany was next. "I'm thankful for three days off of school. And I'm thankful Dad didn't kill me yesterday." Ha. Funny. I didn't know Tiffany was funny. She was so skinny I didn't think she had room for a sense of humor.

My turn. "I'm thankful for turkey, and gravy, and stuffing and sweet potatoes and rolls and green beans with bacon. And I'm glad the Native Americans showed the Pilgrims how to make pie."

Then Mom. "I'm thankful for my three beautiful daughters and my handsome husband, who are going to do all the dishes."

Finally, Dad. He took a sip from his drink and sighed contentedly. "I'm thankful for the four lovely ladies who take care of me every day. But mostly, I'm thankful that we're all really good looking."

It was probably our most perfect Thanksgiving. No one fought. No one cried. No one threw up from eating too much pie.[35] I was doing the dishes and scrubbing the last crumb off the last plate when the phone rang. Oh

---

35. I swear that only happened once. And I was an amateur back then. I can totally handle my pie now.

great. I bet it was a boy calling to take Layla or Tiffany away for the rest of the night. I had almost liked hanging out with them all day. They weren't so bad once you got over the fact that their lips were permanently locked to boys who probably didn't floss.

I listened for Dad to hand the phone off, but he didn't. He just kept talking. I turned the water off so I could hear better. Mom was shaking her head at him, but I guess he didn't see her because he said yes to whoever was on the phone.

"Yeah, that sounds great. Christmas sounds like a great time for a visit."

Visitors! We never got visitors! I was just about to ask who was coming when Dad said, "All right. Good-bye, Mom. Yeah, call me back with the details."

WHAT! Grandmother was visiting? She hadn't been to our house in almost five years, which wasn't weird because we weren't really big on grandparents. Mom's parents had been a long time in heaven and Mom didn't really talk about them. And Dad's dad was a big deal army guy and we never really saw him because Dad didn't really think he was a cool dude. But now his mom was visiting. This was going to be huge. Mostly because I only knew one thing about her: Mom HATED her.

CHAPTER NINE

Mom was a total wreck in the days leading up to Christmas. At night, she cleaned the dickens out of the house. And that was after she cleaned the dickens out of the hotel all day. Things got really weird when she started ironing everything. She ironed the curtains. She ironed the dishtowels. She ironed all of the laundry, even Dad's underpants. And she tried to iron my overalls.[36]

I didn't understand what the big deal was. Dad's mom was visiting, not the Pope. Unless Dad's mom was the Pope, which was highly possible because I didn't really know anything about her. She hadn't visited since I was a little kid. Way before Dad's legs fell all the way asleep.

All I knew was that she lived in Missouri, which sounded Missour-able. Mostly because Mom said she

---

36. While I was still wearing them.

was a complex woman who was never in "a very happy place." I asked why she didn't move to a happier place like Disneyland or the Jelly Belly factory but Mom said it was more complicated than that.

And Dad never had much to say about his own mother at all. Whenever I asked about her, he would change the subject and say, "Do you want some pudding? I would love some pudding." And then I would get us pudding because, well, I was hungrier for butterscotch pudding than I was for information about my own grandmother. Luckily, I knew there was always one person who would give it to me straight no matter what.

I found Tiffany folding towels an hour before Grandmother was scheduled to arrive.

"So what's the deal with the old lady? Do you know anything about her?"

"She's crazy."

"Oh yeah?" I was curious. "What kind of crazy?"

"I don't know much. But it sounds like she went nuts after Grandpa divorced her when Dad was younger. I think Dad wanted to live with Grandpa and that's what really pushed her over the edge."

I combed through the facts in my head while Tiffany folded. Crazy huh? It made sense why Grandmother would have gone crazy way back then but maybe she would be less crazy now that Dad was all grown up. Especially now that Dad and Grandpa didn't talk much. We hadn't seen him in a while either. The last time I saw Grandpa he tried to steal my nose and I was traumatized for life.

I needed more information. "Do you think she's still crazy?"

"Oh yeah. Maybe even crazier."

"Yikes." This didn't sound promising. "Do you think her crazy is genetic? Will we get it?!"

Tiffany looked me up and down like a doctor examining a patient. "I think one of us already has."

I rolled my eyes and walked away. She was totally kidding.[37]

I retired to my room and thought long and hard about how our Christmas was being infiltrated by crazy. Our Christmas, which had already been compromised by Mom telling us we were only getting a few gifts because "things were tight" since Dad left work.

Yeah, things were tight, lady. Including my pants, which was why I needed new ones. And I also needed every Tolkien novel because I saw Clyde reading *The Hobbit* one day and if it meant he was into short people, then maybe I stood a chance. And I also needed an assortment of candies and chocolates to replenish my "for emergencies only" stash that was completely depleted.

~~~~~~~~~~~~~~~

37. RIGHT?!

I pulled a book out from under my pillow and tried to forget about Christmas and everything I wouldn't get. I decided to get lost on Prince Edward Island in the pages of *Anne of Green Gables*.

I must have gotten really lost because I didn't even hear Grandmother arrive. In fact, I didn't hear Mom calling for me to welcome Grandmother. In double fact, I didn't even hear my bedroom door creak open. But eventually the smell of old lady lotion made me look up.

So this was what crazy looked like. She was very small and frail. So frail I imagined her bones were made of dust, so I scooted back trying not to knock her over. Her brown hair was cut super short and her face hung like a bulldog's. The strangest part? She sort of looked like an evil dictator even though I had no reason to believe she was either evil or a dictator. And the brown eyes I thought we shared were actually much darker than mine. Probably muddled by years of crazy this and crazy that. I felt like if I gazed into those dark eyes long enough, I would see all kinds of evil things, but I didn't want to see evil things because I was just a kid, so I gazed at the floor instead.

I was about to ask her all about being crazy, but she spoke first.

"Oh Maggie, what happened to you?"

Her voice was low and gravelly and I must have still been lost on Prince Edward Island because I answered her in my best turn-of-the-century vernacular.

"Whatever do you mean, Grandmother?"

She shook her head. "I'll be speaking to your mother about this." She disappeared out the door and I jumped up and looked in the mirror.

I expected to see a Cyclops eye forming on my forehead or a witch's wart taking over my nose or at the very least I expected to see chocolate evidence from the Mr. Goodbar I had finished just seconds before she opened my door, but there was nothing. I looked like the Maggie I always looked like. What was she talking about?

I headed to the kitchen to investigate and found Mom and Grandmother huddled close in conversation at the counter. Unfortunately, I only caught the tail end of their talk.

"Well, maybe if you were home with your children like a mother should be, this wouldn't have happened," Grandmother lectured. "My children grew up getting three square meals a day."

Mom's face looked like it was going to explode when she noticed me. "Hey Maggie, go wash up for dinner. We're leaving in five minutes."

I pretended to do as she said but I hung back, waiting to hear the rest.

Mom put on her coat. "Listen, you're here to see *your* son. Who could really use a mother right now. Why don't you just leave my children to me?"

She walked away so fast she almost ran right into me. Busted. She took one look at me and pulled me down the hall to my room, where she slammed the door shut.

"The nerve of that woman! You'd think after all we've been through that she would at the very least be cordial! I don't know why I put up with it! She's only been here an hour and already she's ruined everything! How am I going to make it through the next forty-eight hours?!"

Mom collapsed on Tiffany's bed and smooshed a pillow over her face. For a second, she looked just like Tiffany. Bad attitude and all. Then she tossed the pillow to the side and I could see worry fill her from head to toe.

"Maggie! I am so sorry! I shouldn't have reacted like that, especially in front of you. I just—" She looked stuck somewhere between angry and hysterical. "I just totally lost it, didn't I?"

I laughed nervously. "Um, yeah."

She stood up and got my hairbrush from the dresser. "There aren't many people in this world who can get me as worked up as your grandmother." She brushed my hair. "It's just that we have two very different definitions of family."

I liked definitions so I asked, "What do you mean?"

"Well, I want you girls to feel loved every single day. Even when I'm not around I want you to know that I am thinking about you every single second. And I want you to feel like you can come to me for anything, anything at all."

She brushed my hair harder.

"But your grandmother parents through fear and guilt and judgment and—"

"Mom, you're brushing really hard."

Mom released her death grip on the brush. "Sorry, honey. I'm terrible. I shouldn't be talking about your grandmother like this."

"It's okay." I took the brush away. "Tiffany already told me she's crazy."

She looked genuinely relieved. "I'm glad somebody did."

Dinner was weird, to say the least. We went to some fancy-schmancy restaurant that was completely empty because it was Christmas Eve and duh, families not taken over by crazy ate at home on Christmas Eve. Grandmother ordered everyone's meal, even Mom's, which made Mom's freckles boil. My meal was a garden salad with NO DRESSING, which I thought was just an appetizer, but no, it was my whole meal. My WHOLE MEAL was a salad with NO DRESSING.

As soon as we got home, I went straight to my "for emergencies only" stash in my room. But it was just as empty as it was before. I dug into the bottom of my drawer looking for something, anything! And just then, a Rolo rolled out from under a sock.

It was a Christmas miracle!

I woke up the next morning to Tiffany's sideways face staring at me.

"Merry Christmas," she whispered.

"Merry Christmas," I whispered back.

"I'm scared to go out there. It's like having a stranger take over our Christmas."

"She's not a stranger." I sat up. "She's our grandmother."

"You know what I mean."

I did. I knew exactly what she meant.

She halfway smiled. "But it *is* kind of fun watching Mom lose it."

"Yeah, it is," I agreed.

We promised each other we wouldn't go out into the living room alone so I waited for Tiffany while she did whatever she does for an hour in the bathroom. When she finally emerged done up in red, green, and glitter, we slowly made our way into the living room.

Dad was at the table drinking coffee with Grandmother while Mom and Layla were busy in the kitchen fixing a Christmas feast. The tree was ablaze with colored lights and brightly wrapped gifts for one and all. I suppressed my urge to dive into the presents immediately and found Mom instead.

I squeezed her side. "Merry Christmas."

She smiled. "What took you so long? You have a million presents to open!"

There weren't a million presents but there were definitely more than I expected. Mom had made it sound like we were only getting socks and gruel for Christmas. But I got everything I needed and even a few things I didn't, like a brass bookmark from Mom and a Neil Young record from Dad.

Even Tiffany and Layla got me a present, which was a Mayfield family first. I unwrapped the tiny box, lifted the lid, and ta-da! Inside was the most perfect pair of fake diamond earrings. They were dainty and understated. Former First Lady Jacqueline Kennedy would have approved.

"They're so pretty!" I held them up to see their sparkle. "But my ears aren't pierced."

Layla pushed my hair behind my ears. "Mom said we could take you to get them pierced."

I shivered at the thought. "Maybe. I'll think about it."

My turn. I reached under the tree for the two gifts I'd wrapped especially for my sisters. I could barely contain my excitement as I handed one to Tiffany and one to Layla. They tore open the paper and tried to hide their disappointment.

"Books," Layla said flatly.

Tiffany examined her book like she'd never seen one before.

"Love poems to be exact," I said. "Elizabeth Barrett Browning wrote them for her husband who was also a poet. I thought you would really like them. Since they're about love. And stuff."

Their faces lit up and Layla gave me a squeeze. "This is great, Maggie."

"Yeah, this doesn't suck. Entirely," Tiffany agreed.

"I'm so glad you like them. They're due back to the library next Monday. Don't be late. Mom gets really mad when she has to pay overdue charges."

Layla and Tiffany laughed and Mom and Dad laughed and Grandmother just sat there because crazy people only laugh to themselves in secret while they're cooking up crazy plans to do all sorts of crazy things. It almost seemed like a normal Christmas. Then Grandmother handed Dad her gift.

I honestly wasn't expecting her to give him much. I mean she'd only given Mom a box of cologne. She'd given Layla and Tiffany lip gloss sets and me a nightgown that was four sizes too small. So her gifts were under the top, to say the least.

She gave Dad an envelope and watched him open it. Her face looked intense and even crazier than usual.

He pulled out a business card. "What is this, Mom?"

"It's the card of the top neurologist in Saint Louis. The wait to see him is usually a year long, but I did some pushing and managed to get you in the week after next. He'll get you all fixed up. He's the best of the best."

Dad was silent. We were all silent because Dad was silent. And then Dad flipped.

"No one is going to fix me up, Mom. Don't you listen? I've told you over and over again. Now drop it!"

"Don't raise your voice at me!" Grandmother said while raising her voice. "I'm just trying to help. I'm just trying to talk some sense into you. I brought you up to be more responsible than this. You haven't thought through a single thing!"

"Mom! I've done all the research. I've seen all the best doctors. I know what I'm doing!"

"Oh you do, do you?" Grandmother lost it.[38] "This from the man who quits his job out of nowhere. You had twenty-five years with that company. And you just threw it all away! You can't take care of your family, let alone yourself!"

"That's enough!" Dad locked eyes with hers. "And I mean it!"

Mom stepped in. "Girls. Go to your rooms."

The three of us stood up together but Dad wanted us to sit back down. "No, stay. *Stay.*"

Mom looked worried. "Honey, I don't think now is the time to—"

"I'd like to say something. To my family."

Dad locked his wheels in front of Grandmother. "Now, I appreciate your concern. But I am getting the very best care here. Dale and the girls—"

"Dale and the girls don't know the first thing about taking care of you! If you'd been given the proper care and attention all along you wouldn't be in this condition!"

"This is just like you! You don't listen!" Dad shouted. "And then you just say all of these horrible things and

---

38. Even more so than she already had.

you think there are no consequences! Well, I can say horrible things too, Mom. Where have you been? The past eleven years. *Where have you been?* You hate Dad but you're just like him. Both of you just ran away."

"I won't stand for this." Grandmother stood up even though she just said she wouldn't. "Not on Christmas." She stormed off.

Dad yelled after her, "That makes two of us!"

Grandmother stayed locked in Layla's room the rest of the night. We tried to carry on with Christmas but it felt super weird. Mom even tried to get Grandmother to come out for dinner but she refused. And I was glad she did. That meant more peace for my family and more honey-baked ham for me.

The next day Mom took her to the airport before any of us woke up. All she left behind was a bottle of her old lady lotion that I buried in the back of the linen closet. Far away from my family but close enough so if I ever needed to be reminded what crazy smelled like, I could take a sniff.

Before I knew it, it was New Year's Eve and my family was a family again. Mom made us black-eyed peas to eat for luck on New Year's Day and Dad lined up a stack of records he wanted to listen to as we rang in the new year. And I thought long and hard about my New Year's resolution. The year before I had resolved to make myself a scholarly triple threat by getting straight As, perfect attendance, and at least one academic award. I had succeeded effortlessly. But after everything that had happened, I resolved to do something that might have seemed impossible, especially to Dad. I resolved to do something that would take all of my brain, all of my heart, and both my bootstraps pulled all the way up.

I resolved to fix Dad.

CHAPTER TEN

The first week back to school after Christmas break is always thrilling. But this time I was going to try even more to give it my all. Maybe I was excited to learn more and more so I could get smarter and smarter and closer and closer to fixing Dad. Maybe I just needed a distraction after everything that happened with Grandmother. Or maybe I was just the smartest kid in my entire class.[39] I was on an academic roll and by Thursday afternoon my arm was drained of blood from raising it so much.

I was about to give my arm a rest and let someone else answer, when Mrs. Nicol asked, "Who refused to give up her seat on an Alabama bus?"

No one raised their hand. FOOLS. I eagerly raised mine.

Mrs. Nicol sighed. "Anyone other than Maggie?"

---

39. Yep, that had to be it.

I meekly lowered my hand and Mrs. Nicol called on Mary Winter (the class airhead).

After about a million "ums," Mary said, "Florence Nightingale?"

Seriously? Am I the only one who did her homework even when we didn't have homework? I was just about to redeem my generation by yelling "Rosa Parks" when the bell rang.

I was up and at 'em the next morning. I'd read four chapters ahead in my history book the night before so I felt confident knowing I knew more than usual. I was only going to read two chapters ahead but then the civil rights movement took off and I had to know if Lyndon B. Johnson got his act together. I was zipping my book bag up when Mom unexpectedly appeared at my door.

"Why aren't you at work, lady?"

"Stop calling me lady, *lady*," she said with a look. "I took the day off to spend with my girls. How do you feel about a little adventure?"

"Well, maybe later. I'm staying after school to clean the erasers."

"Why do you have to do that? Did you get in trouble?"

"Trouble? I volunteered. I consider it my civic duty."

She looked impressed and worried at the same time. "Okay, well, you're going to have to miss it today. We're going to play hooky. Doesn't that sound cool?"

Was she kidding? It sounded the opposite of cool. "I can't skip school. What if I miss a pop quiz or something?"

Mom held out my coat. "I already checked with your teachers. Missing a day is fine."

I objected big time. "No way, Mom!"

She pushed me out the door.

"This is kidnapping!"

Next thing I knew, I was bundled up and being forced into the car next to Tiffany who was already buckled up. Layla was in the front seat. Was she really kidnapping all three of us?

"I don't want to be kidnapped!" I screamed.

Mom looked at me in the rearview mirror. "It's perfectly legal to kidnap your own children."

"We'll let the court of law decide that." I nodded at Tiffany, who was staring at me with her nose wrinkled.

"You're so weird."

And just like that we were driving down the highway with the radio blasting ON A SCHOOL DAY. I gave everyone the silent treatment. Mostly because I was mad and partly because when you're kidnapped, you're not supposed to give your captors any reason to dislike you.

Layla checked her mascara in the passenger mirror. "Come on Maggie, cheer up! Today is going to be fun!"

"How do you know? Have you been conspiring with the enemy?"

Mom didn't like that. At all. "I'll have you know, Magnolia Jane Mayfield"—uh-oh. She used my whole name. Trouble—"your sisters and I planned this entire day just for you. So be nice and get excited."

"Actually they planned it," said Tiffany. "I was forced to come along against my will."

I held out my hand for her to shake in solidarity but she refused it and went back to layering on lip gloss.[40]

"How am I supposed to be excited if I don't even know where we're going?"

Mom pulled into a parking lot lined with giant trees. "We're here. The High Museum of Art." She turned around and smiled. "Excited now?"

The place was huge and overwhelming and totally exciting.

"We're going on a full tour of museums today," Mom explained. "This is our first stop and then we're going to the Atlanta History Center. It's time you saw some real history, instead of just reading about it in school."

"This is awesome!" I yelled louder than you're supposed to yell in front of museums. I lowered my voice back to normal. "Is Dad meeting us here?"

~~~~~~~~~~~~~~

40. The amount of time and effort my sisters put into their looks is really astounding. I bet if you added it all up, they've both spent 80 to 85% of their lives shellacking on Bonne Bell Lip Smackers.

"No, honey," Mom said. "We're going to have a great time. It'll be just us girls."

I was skeptical. A girls' day? They better not make me shop for anything. Unless it's a Picasso.

Mom bought our tickets and we turned through the turnstiles and went back in time. I hadn't thought I was really into art. I mean the only art we did in art class involved Popsicle sticks but no Popsicles and that just seemed wrong. But this art jumped off every wall. There were so many colors, so many faces, so many naked people I wasn't supposed to see but Mom said they were like the naked people in *National Geographic* so it was okay. Layla loved the Degas dancers and Tiffany loved the Renoir lady and I loved this painting of raspberries that I imagined were sugared like Mom always made them.

We *oohed* and *aahed* for an hour and then Mom said it was time to go to our next destination. On our way to the car, we passed a wishing well.

Layla pushed Mom for coins. "Come on, Mom. You have to have a penny in your purse somewhere."

Mom's arm disappeared into her bag and came back out holding three pennies. "You're in luck!" She handed one to each of us. "Make it count."

Layla tossed hers in first and probably made a wish about being senior prom queen. Tiffany was next and she probably made a wish about being junior prom queen.

I handed my penny back to Mom. "Here, you throw it. I don't want to."

"Oh come on, Maggie," she said. "You have to make a wish."

"I'm pretty sure it's illegal to throw wishes in there and I can't break a law. I'm going to be president one day! How many times do I have to tell you?!"

She laughed. "Okay, okay. I'll make a wish then."

She held on super tight to the penny and let it go behind her without opening her eyes. She looked like she was wishing really hard. She was probably wishing for . . . Hmmm, I didn't know what Mom wished for. She never really wanted anything. I would've asked her but I didn't want her to give up her wish by telling me. I wanted it to come true. Whatever it was.

We drove down busy city streets and made our way to the History Center. Inside, I took a deep breath that smelled the way smart felt. Mom and I walked side by side and she guided us through the civil rights exhibition while Layla and Tiffany pretended to pay attention.

"I remember this." Mom pointed at a picture of Martin Luther King Jr. walking down an Atlanta street surrounded by people. "He was a great man. Gone way too soon."

"Did you go to the parade he was in?" I asked.

"Oh, it wasn't a parade. It was a march on Washington. I didn't go, but I watched it on TV with my dad and it was so exciting. That time was really electric, you know?"

I questioned her hippie vocabulary. "Electric?"

"Yes, electric. Like *alive*. Like things were finally changing for the better even though sometimes it was scary. Especially growing up down here. Atlanta was the center of it all because of Dr. King. And living here, you really felt like you were a part of it. A part of the change."

I searched the photos for electricity and swore I saw a spark here and there. "I'm going to make history one day too, you know."

Mom smiled. "You already are."

We walked and walked around some more until our legs were too full of history to walk anymore. So we headed for the car. I couldn't wait to get home and tell Dad all about our day. We piled into the car and then Mom laid another surprise on me.

"Guess what? The adventure isn't over yet. I booked us a room at the hotel, and we're going to spend the night in a fancy suite. How does that sound, Maggie?"

I had to admit. It sounded exciting. But it also sounded fiscally irresponsible. "I dunno, Mom. Sounds expensive."

"That's the best part," Mom said. "I traded a day off for a room for the night. It's not going to cost a thing."

"But we don't have our pajamas."

"You don't give me enough credit, Maggie. I had Layla pack you a bag last night."

"What? What did you pack for me?" I had to know.

"Don't worry," Layla said. "I have your Rise and Shine nightgown."

"And what else?"

"And your GIGANTIC old lady underpants." She laughed.

I defended my own honor. "They're not gigantic, okay? I just like having room to move around."

When we got to the hotel, I expected Dad to be waiting for us in the lobby but he was nowhere to be found.

"When is Dad getting here?" I asked. "Did you send the fancy hotel limo to get him?"

"It's just us for the night," Mom explained. "Dad's staying at home."

"He's what?!" My yell bounced off every inch of marble in the lobby.

"Shhh," Mom lowered her voice. "He's fine. David[41] is staying at the house. He's sleeping on the couch. They are probably watching football and yelling at the TV right now."

This didn't make any sense. "But who's going to make him dinner and finish his ice cream and help him brush his teeth and pick him up and put him in bed?!"

"David can do all that. Trust me." She grabbed a key from a hand I could barely see over the tall front desk. "Now, let's go check out our room."

~~~~~~~~~~~~~~~~~

41. David is Dad's very best friend. He works at the airport like Dad and has a mustache like Dad and likes Budweiser and hippie music like Dad.

We rode up the glass elevator in silence.

But the silence was over when Mom opened the door to our room.

"There are only two beds!" Tiffany yelled.

Mom put our bags in the closet. "Yes, you and Maggie are sleeping in one bed and Layla and I are sleeping in the other."

Great, I shared a room with Tiffany at home and now I had to share a bed with her here? This was supposed to be a break from the daily grind. And my daily grind had a ponytail and legs that karate kicked at night. When Tiffany lay down on the bed her giraffe arms and legs nearly took up the whole thing. I'd be lucky if I made it through the night alive.

I was going to stay mad, but then Mom made up for it.

"How about room service for dinner?"

I snatched the menu out of her hands. "I'll take the pancakes. And a hamburger. And a steak."

Mom took the menu back. "We're going to pick a couple things and share them."

"FINE," I huffed in a very unfine way. Even though it was actually fine. We ordered two hamburgers, two orders of fries, and four Coca-Colas and feasted while watching *Entertainment Tonight*.

Like always, I was the last to get in the bathroom. I brushed my teeth and put on my favorite nightgown that Layla packed for me. I had to admit, she had good taste.

When I walked back into the room, she was just hanging up the phone.

"Geez, Layla, can't you spend one whole day away from Bobby? It's not like you can make out through the phone."

She threw a pillow. At my head.

"It wasn't Bobby. It was Dad."

"Hey, call him back! I want to say good night."

"No, Maggie," Mom said. "It's time for bed and Dad's really tired. We'll see him in the morning."

I never understood why a guy who sat down all day was always so tired at night. But I didn't fight her to call him back. I was tired too from all the seeing and thinking. I crawled into bed with Tiffany, who promptly rolled over and scared the BEEGEEZUS out of me.

"Something's eating your face!" I screamed.

"It's a face mask. It's going to keep me beautiful," she said without moving her lips.

I shook my head. "Good luck with that."

The next day we packed up and headed home after breakfast. I couldn't wait to tell Dad all about our adventures. I wanted to be the first to see him, so I ran into the house, rushed down the hall, opened his door, and ta-da!

He was sleeping. At one in the afternoon. On a Saturday.

Sure, I didn't have reason to believe he wasn't always asleep in the afternoon. Who knew what he did while I was at school? But it seemed strange. I tiptoed over to his bed and he shook awake.

"Hey, Mags. How was your trip? Did you have fun?"

His eyes were half-awake and half—somewhere else and they weren't smiling like they usually did. His face wasn't smiling either. In fact, he kind of looked like . . . well, he kind of looked like he was in pain.

Something was wrong. Really wrong. I looked around the room for his wheelchair and found it locked in place next to the door. There were no new scratches or dings. So I didn't think he'd toppled over again. And there were no dropped forks around his bed so I knew that wasn't getting him down. Still, whatever had happened while we were away was a big deal.

I wanted to yell at him. I wanted to scream. I wanted to know what was going on, but when I brushed the hair out of his eyes, I saw the tired that had taken over his whole face. And I couldn't yell. I couldn't scream. All I could do was swallow the lump in my throat.

I resisted my first instinct, which was to call for Mom. I don't know why I didn't. Maybe I didn't want her to see Dad like this. Maybe if only I saw him like this then I could figure out a way to make him better before anyone else knew. I stopped thinking and followed my second instinct. I leaned over and hugged him. I squeezed him. And when we both let go, I noticed something on his wrist.

He was wearing a hospital bracelet.

CHAPTER ELEVEN

"Dad?" I tugged at the hospital bracelet. "What is this?" My voice was calm. Even though my brain was screaming.

He could tell I was upset. "Okay, okay. You caught me." He called for Mom, "Honey, can you come in here?"

She appeared and Dad smiled weakly. "Why don't we tell Maggie what's going on?"

I crossed my arms. "Yeah. Why don't we tell Maggie what's going on?"

Mom frowned at me. "Hey, no attitude, okay?"

"Yes ma'am," I said under my breath. I crawled into bed with Dad.

Mom pulled the covers up over both of us and sat down on the side of the bed. "Dad's doctors thought a new medicine might make him stronger. And he had to get it right away. So that's why we left in such a hurry."

"But why didn't you just tell me that?"

"There wasn't any time," Mom said.

"What kind of medicine?"

"A really powerful one. It's a kind of steroid," Dad answered.

"Aren't those illegal? Are you breaking the law?!"

"No, no," Mom said. "These are the safe and legal kind. They are going to give Dad a little pick-me-up. And there might be a few side effects."

"What's a side effect?"

"It's something bad that can pop up when you're trying to make things better," Mom explained.

"Like how my stunted growth is a side effect of sharing a room with Tiffany."

Mom shook her head. "You're growing just fine, Maggie."

"I meant my emotional growth, Mom."

Dad laughed, which was nice to hear, but I wasn't finished.

"So why did he go to the hospital?"

"Well, this medicine is very special and can only be given at the hospital. And it takes a long time to get all the medicine, so Dad stayed in the hospital overnight."

"What? Dad stayed in the hospital overnight?! Why didn't we stay with him?"

Dad looked down. He straightened his left fingers with his right fingers and it looked like he was holding his own hand. "I didn't want you girls to worry."

I put his hand in mine. "But that's our job."

He squeezed my hand with his. "No, Maggie. That's *my* job."

I felt scared and kind of the same way I'd felt when we found Dad on the floor and again when he dropped his fork. And I hated that feeling. I hated it more than I hated anything in the world including Brussels sprouts and acorn squash. Man, I hated acorn squash.

I scooted over to get out of the bed. "I'm going to get Layla and Tiffany. They should know about this."

Mom stopped me. "They already do."

I didn't understand. "How? We just got home."

"I told Tiffany this morning. And we told Layla the night before."

That's when I pitched a fit. I pitched a fit even though I'd never pitched a fit before.

Sure, I threw tantrums here and there as a kid, but mostly Tiffany was the fit pitcher in our family. Every other day (and sometimes hour) she'd scream, "Why can't I stay out past ten?!" "Why can't I dye my hair pink?!" "Why can't I join a weirdo band of gypsies and travel from seedy town to seedy town with a muscle man and bearded lady?!"

Okay, she never shouted that last one, but I could see it coming. She was always filled with so much teenage rage, and I never wanted to be like her. I never wanted to lose my mind. Plus, I was more mature than her. And grown-ups don't fight. They debate.

But the anger I felt right then wasn't debatable. It was boiling and I couldn't stop it from exploding. I yelled one yell after the next. Why did they keep this from me?! Why did they blatantly LIE to me?! Why did they tell Layla and Tiffany everything and me nothing when I was the one with the perfect GPA? I was the one with the off-the-charts critical thinking skills. I was the one who was going to change the whole wide world one day. I was going to be president. To be commander-in-chief. And they wouldn't even let me be a leader in my own house!

"You're right, Maggie," Mom finally admitted. "You're totally right."

I wasn't finished. "I don't even know who you two are anymore!"

"Don't be so dramatic," Mom said. "Parents make mistakes sometimes."

"Tell me about it!" I yelled. In a *tone*.

I wrapped my scarf tight around my neck and got back into bed with Dad. I unfolded his arm to get into his nook so we could watch whatever movie I wanted because I deserved to get whatever I wanted. When I pulled on his arm, he winced and I saw that on the opposite side of his elbow his arm was the most *purple* purple I'd ever seen.

I bit my lip. "Does it hurt?"

"A little, but I'm a big tough guy, remember?"

I laughed even though I didn't want to laugh. It was what I liked most about Dad. He was funny. Even when he wasn't supposed to be.

I pulled myself close to his side. "I love you, Dad."

He used his unpurple arm to pull his purple arm around my shoulder. "I love you more, Maggie."

I was mad.

To say the least.

Every member of my family had lied to me. They intentionally kept a secret from me. An important secret that so many others knew before me.

Dad knew.

Mom knew.

Layla knew.

Tiffany knew.

David knew.

The nurses who took care of Dad knew.

The doctors who listened to Dad's heart knew.

The parking lot attendant at the hospital knew.

The hospital bracelet maker knew.

The Garfield Band-Aid giver knew.

Would I ever be able to trust any of them again? I sulked and pondered and wondered and ignored my family for days and days. Mom tried to make amends with chocolate.

"I made a batch of Toll House cookies just for you. Want one?"

I shook my head, escaped into my room, waited for the coast to be clear, and then belly crawled into the kitchen, stole two from the still-warm plate, and escaped again.

What? I didn't see any reason why the cookies should suffer. It wasn't their fault she couldn't be trusted.

Dad tried to trick me with TV. "Oh wow," he yelled. "MY FAVORITE MOVIE *PIPPI LONGSTOCKING* IS ON! I WISH SOMEONE WOULD WATCH IT WITH ME."

No dice. I didn't need Pippi's problems. I had my own.

Tiffany didn't even try to talk to me, which wasn't a surprise. We were in a war long before this. It was a lot like the Cold War only it wasn't really cold because Dad always kept the thermostat at a balmy seventy-eight degrees.

I was sure I would never talk to any of them again. I was prepared to secede from our family and start my own across the masking tape border in my room. In fact, I was working on the design of my new family crest when Layla came in and collapsed on my bed.

"I need to know everything you know about Atticus Finch."

"Good luck." I turned away from her and focused all my attention on my notebook.

"Come on," she pleaded. "It's life or death."

I raised an eyebrow.

"Okay, it's life or death for my English paper."

"Have you even read *To Kill a Mockingbird*? It's probably the easiest book in the world to understand. Even for you."

"Yes, I read it! And I even understood it. I'm not an idiot, you know?"

I felt kind of bad for implying that she was.

"Come on, help me. I just finished my horrible biology homework and I don't have any brainpower left for this."

She looked genuinely desperate. So I decided to help her.

"What do you need to know?"

"Ah! Yes! You're the best!" She hugged me. "I need to write about three traits that make Atticus Finch a strong and complex character."

"That's easy. Is your pencil sharpened?"

She nodded yes and I stood like all great orators stand and I clasped my hands behind my back like all great orators do and I paced because great orators pace.

"First things first. Atticus Finch was a man of great integrity. He wasn't afraid to do something he believed in even if it meant putting everything on the line. Not only did he have integrity, he believed that every man should. That's why he defended Tom Robinson."

"This is great, Maggie," Layla said without looking up from her notebook. "Keep going."

"He wasn't a showman or a showboater or a show—anything else. He was a quiet hero. Which you don't come across often, you know? Heroes are always these big deal guys with muscles who love talking about themselves. But not Atticus. He was above all that."

She nodded. "Cool, I just need one more."

"Hmmm, well, I guess if there was one more thing to say about him it would be that he taught by example. Jem and Scout learned that he always had honest intentions even if he wasn't always honest with them. He was just the most stand-up guy ever."

"I can see that." She nodded. "He seemed like a really cool dad. But don't tell Dad I said that. He always says he's the coolest."

I shook my head with certainty. "Our dad has *nothing* on Atticus Finch."

"Yeah, I don't think Atticus Finch ever got arrested for stage diving." She laughed.

"Even if he did, he would never have told his kids about it!"

"Dad's all about the TMI."

"TMI?" I asked.

"Too much information."

"That's great. Yeah, Dad is all about the TMI."

"But come on, you have to admit. He's pretty brave."

I shrugged. "I guess."

But she didn't let it go. "Maggie, you're too scared to get your ears pierced. Look what's happening to him. It's way scarier. Just think about it."

No one had ever really told me to think. Because, well, I was always thinking. Telling me to think was like telling me to breathe. It was like telling my hair to grow, my heart to beat, my bones to get bonier. But I took a moment and I thought long and hard about what she said. And my thoughts led me to the truth. I had been so preoccupied with what had happened to ME. How I had been lied to, betrayed, and backstabbed by my own family. It consumed me so much that I hadn't, not even once, thought about what was happening to DAD.

I considered all the brave people throughout history and literature. What did Dad have in common with them? Abraham Lincoln and Dad both had unruly heads of hair but the comparison stopped there. Dad and Franklin Roosevelt were both in wheelchairs but Dad didn't end a world war from his. The closest he ever got to revolution was demanding that Mom stop trying to switch him to decaf.

But when I thought about it some more, Dad did have something in common with all of these bravest of brave people. Abraham Lincoln, Franklin Roosevelt, Anne Frank, Dr. King, Rosa Parks, Amelia Earhart, Atticus Finch, and my dad, Dan Mayfield: They never, ever gave up.

I thought about things. A LOT. And maybe it was time for me to let it all go. Maybe it was time to forgive my family. Yes, Dad had lied to me and that was a huge deal, but he had apologized. Mom had too. I just wasn't ready to hear it. And I couldn't be mad at Layla, because she was just an innocent bystander. But I could be mad at Tiffany because, well, I was always mad at Tiffany.

Layla stood up to leave. "Thanks so much, really. You saved my life."

"Anytime."

I wrapped my scarf around my neck and followed her out of my room and into the living room where Dad was on the phone. He sounded better than ever.

"Yeah doc, I'm feeling good. I don't think I'll win any bodybuilding competitions. But I definitely feel stronger."

I gave him a smile, my first one in four days, and he smiled back. Then I headed for the kitchen where Mom was making dinner.

"Hey, Mom." I made my peace. "What's up?"

She looked surprised. "She finally speaks."

I half-smiled. "Is there anything I can do to help?"

I meant in life. But she thought I meant for dinner. "Yeah, you can set the table. Dinner's almost ready."

I reached for the plates and Mom helped me carry all five of them down to the counter with one hand. I always forgot how strong she was. I gathered the forks and knives and for the first time in days I didn't want to throw them at anybody. I wasn't so angry anymore, but there was something I needed to know.

"Hey, Mom. The other day at the museum . . ." I hesitated. Suddenly I felt like I was asking too much. But

I really needed to know. "What did you wish for at the wishing well?"

Her eyes told me everything.

I knew she had wished for the medicine to work.

"Go get your sisters, okay? It's time to eat."

I knocked on Layla's door and she actually answered. "Hey Maggie, come in."

This had never happened. In my whole life. Layla had never let me into her room. I walked through the door and the smell of hairspray and perfume almost knocked me out. There were magazines all over the place and torn-out pictures of rock stars taped all over the walls. The rock stars were wearing just as much makeup as Tiffany did. Weird. Clothes were EVERYWHERE and I mean EVERYWHERE. I tiptoed away from a bra that was freaking me out.

"It's time for dinner."

She fixed a rogue hair in the mirror. "I'll be right there."

"Hey, um . . ." I knew what I wanted to say but I had a hard time figuring out how to say it. "You didn't really need my help with your homework, did you?"

She turned and wrapped my scarf in a fancy bow around my neck. "Of course I did. You're the smartest girl alive, right?"

"Well . . ." I stared at my feet and spoke under my breath. "Maybe not all the time."

All five of us dined on dinner and all five of us spoke, even me. It was nice, but it wasn't like the good old days. And I was starting to think it never would be again.

I looked over at Dad and saw that most purple of purple bruises finally beginning to fade away. It reminded me that I wasn't any closer to fixing Dad. I knew eventually the bruises would disappear completely but the memory of it wouldn't. I would always remember that purple.

But I wasn't going to lose hope. I wasn't going to give up. Because brave people never, ever give up.

CHAPTER TWELVE

But boy, did I wish I could give up February. I HATED February. It was always gloomy and cold and all anybody talked about was love and smooching and blah blah blah. I hated it. Sure, I got a giant yellow Whitman's Sampler from Dad. Sure, Layla and Tiffany would let me have theirs. Sure, there was candy at school every day. But there were also Flower-Grams and I HATED Flower-Grams.

Never heard of a Flower-Gram? I hadn't either before middle school. But turns out they're a form of torture where boys pay a dollar to have the Booster Club deliver a flower to the girl of their dreams during homeroom. And so what, I probably wasn't going to get one. I probably wasn't ever going to get smallpox either and I considered myself lucky. And so what, maybe I thought Clyde might send me one after we totally had a moment over Neil Young. Even though we hadn't really talked since. So it was totally fine that he didn't. He probably thought they were stupid. Of course he did.[42]

The big delivery day was Valentine's Day. And I made sure not to wear pink or red because I knew every girl in school would be wearing pink or red. So I wore Dad's Bruce Springsteen shirt instead. I didn't need love. I had America.

When I got to my locker, Mary Winter[43] was holding a bouquet of Flower-Grams like they were a Nobel Peace Prize or something. She fixed her hair in her full-length locker mirror and proceeded to ruin my life.

"Happy Valentine's Day Maggie! How many Flower-Grams did you get?"

"I don't believe in flower murder," I said.

"Oh well, I have a bunch if you change your mind. You can have one of mine."

She tried to give me a carnation but I shooed it away. "No, thanks."

She insisted. "Come on, take this one. It's so pretty." She read the tag, which was amazing because I didn't think she could read. "It's from some boy named Clyde? Do you know him?"

~~~~~~~~~~~~~~~

42. God, we were perfect for each other.

43. Turns out whenever Mary Winter was called on in any class, her answer was always "Florence Nightingale." Even in math. I guess she knew, statistically speaking, she'd be right eventually.

HOLY.

WHAT.

I slammed my locker door and ran down the hall with a knife in my heart.

The rest of the day was a blur of one devastation after the next. First the flower and then the cafeteria ran out of chocolate milk and then I got a 94 on my French test instead of my anticipated 98 and then the hand dryer in the bathroom was broken and I had to dry my hands on my pants which left behind an embarrassing wet spot that I didn't want to talk about and then TO TOP IT ALL OFF at the end of the day, that stupid flower was stuck in my locker with a note from Mary that read, "From me to you, Happy Valentine's Day Girl!" *Girl*?! Don't call me *girl*, GIRL. I am a woman. A future world leader. You would never call Margaret Thatcher *GIRL*, would you? Certainly not to her face? ON THE WORST DAY OF HER LIFE?!

When I got home I didn't even want to catch up on current events with Dad. He usually told me all about the news of the day but I couldn't handle any more news. I had enough to deal with. So I went straight to my room and locked the door. But then I realized my Whitman's Sampler was on the table so I went back out, got it, ignored Dad's plea to share it with him, went back to my room, and locked the door again. I collapsed on my bed and cried and cried and ate the Messenger Boy chocolate and then cried some more and ate the Cashew Cluster and then cried some more and thought I was going to throw up so I ate the Mint Crème because mint soothes your tummy.

Why hadn't Clyde sent me a Flower-Gram? Was it my hair? No way. I had perfect hair. Was it my face? Impossible. I had Dad's face and he was the best looking person ever. Was he intimidated by my intelligence? Blinded by my ambition? Maybe it was the quarter inch I had grown over Christmas? I was spiraling even farther down into a deep dark place when someone knocked on my door.

It wasn't a low knock, which meant it wasn't Dad. And it wasn't Layla or Tiffany because they were on dates. Of course they were on dates. It had to be Mom. I opened the door.

She looked excited. "Maggie, someone just called for you!"

What?! I yelled, "Was it Clyde?"

"No, it was your principal. You're student of the month!"

Great. I was student of the month for the month I hated with every fiber of my being. I turned and fell back onto my bed into a sea of chocolate wrappers.

Mom raised an eyebrow as she took in the mess. "Are you okay? Dad said he thought something was wrong. Who's Clyde? Is this about him?"

I smooshed my face into a pillow. "He's NO ONE."

She sat on the bed without asking permission. "Do you want to talk about it?"

I smooshed my face farther into the pillow. "No. I just want to be alone. WITH MY THOUGHTS."

"Okay, well I'm sure Tiffany won't be home for a while. So you'll have the room all to yourself."

Great. The last thing I wanted to think about was Tiffany sucking face with some boy. I turned my head so I could breathe and watched her pick my clothes up off the floor like moms always do.

"Mr. Shoemaker said the student of the month breakfast is Friday. Remember what a great time we had last year?"

She was right. We did have a great time last year. We'd hobnobbed with two of my favorite teachers who had gone on and on about how I was their favorite student and how they were going to miss me and I'd reminded them to remember me when *60 Minutes* called to interview them during my election. It had been a banner morning. Plus, there were assorted jams. And muffins and toast and croissants, which are French for "delicious."

I sat up. "You'll be there, right?"

"Wouldn't miss it for the world."

After she left, I pulled up my bootstraps and reminded myself of my mantra: "Career first. Love second." Forget Clyde. Forget Mary Winter. I would be in the Ivy League soon and they would be in some dumber league like the Weed League or the AstroTurf League.

I had to remember that being student of the month was a really big deal and never got old even though I won it every year. One year I even won twice when the girl who was supposed to be student of the month got caught cheating on a pop quiz. Her loss was my victory. I just needed to move on and stop being so crazy. Especially since there were crazy genes lurking in my bloodstream. I didn't want to activate them. Future world leaders couldn't be crazy.

The next few days were tough but I muscled through and I avoided Mary Winter and Clyde and any thought of the two of them together. And by Friday, my focus was restored and I was ready to receive my student of the month honor with pride.

I rushed off the bus and into school and saved Mom and me the very best seats in the cafeteria. Mom had to go to work first but she swore she'd meet me in the lunchroom at nine o'clock on the dot.

The tables were covered in fancy white crepe paper and vases of flowers sat in the middle of each one. Vases of flowers that included carnations, which I hated less when they were honoring achievement, not love. I waited and waited as the other parents piled in and I got worried my backpack wasn't going to be enough to hold her place.

What was taking her so long? Was she stuck in traffic? Did she forget? No. She would never forget. Finally, just as Mr. Shoemaker was closing the door, one last person arrived. But it wasn't Mom. It was Layla.

She rushed over to the table, picked up my backpack

and took Mom's seat. My jaw dropped. And not just because I was opening it for a croissant.

She unfolded her napkin in her lap and whispered, "Did I miss anything?"

Did she miss anything? What the heck was *I* missing?

"Where's Mom?" I hissed as I pulled the jam bowl away from her.

"She's stuck at work, so she sent me. You're not mad, are you?"

"Mad? Mad? Of course I'm mad!" I whisper-yelled. "Mom said she wouldn't miss this for the world!" What was she, some kind of world hater?

"Shh, Maggie. She couldn't make it, so I'm here. Okay?"

"This is great. This is just *great.*"

Mr. Shoemaker started the breakfast with an orange juice toast to me and my fellow students of the month, each from a different grade. He called each of us up one at a time to get our certificate. And everyone paused and posed for a picture. And their moms and dads applauded their hands off. And I was the only one without a parent applauding. Geez Louise.

I ate my strawberry jammed biscuit in silence while Layla mingled with the parents. She laughed at their unfunny jokes and answered all of their questions and looked perfect and on my second grape jammed biscuit, she turned to me.

"This is great, Maggie. You're doing really well here. Way better than me. I hated middle school."

"You hate all school," I said with a perfectly timed roll of my eyes.

"That's not true," she defended herself. "I like high school. But in middle school, I just got made fun of."

I actually stopped chewing and looked at her. "Yeah right."

She took the teeniest amount of orange marmalade and spread it on her toast. "I did. You don't remember me back then? I guess you were really little. I was so skinny I looked like a skeleton and kids were so mean and ugh, I begged Mom to let me stay home from school every day."

"Really?" I asked.

"Really," she said.

"Well, when did you get so popular?"

"I'm not popular," Layla said. "Actually, everyone thinks I'm a goody-goody."

Now I was interested. "No way."

"Yes way. I may not be as good at school as you, but I do try really hard. I just really suck at math. And science. And English," she continued. "And history," she added with a laugh. "And French."

"I can help anytime, you know."

"Thanks. That would be great."

The weirdest part? She was starting to feel less like my bossy big sister who hogged the bathroom and constantly left the curling iron on. She felt like more of a friend who was also a bossy big sister who hogged the bathroom and constantly left the curling iron on.

Layla checked her makeup in her hand mirror and I nudged her with my elbow.

"Hey, thanks for coming. I'm sure you didn't want to."

"Thanks for letting me stay. It was fun," she said. "Mom's really bummed she missed it, you know."

"I guess," I muttered.

"I'm serious, Maggie." She lifted my chin up and took a good look at me. "Hold on a sec." She pulled out a tiny jar from her bag and dotted some strawberry lip gloss on my lips.

"Yep, that's definitely your color. Do you want it?"

"Really?"

She folded my fingers over the jar of gloss. "It's all yours. But you have to pinky swear you'll wipe it off every day before you get home from school."

I wrapped my pinky around hers and squeezed.

"I don't want to be the one to corrupt you." She winked. "That's Tiffany's job."

By the final bell I had gone a little crazy but not like on Valentine's Day. I had gone a little crazy with the lip gloss. I had a strawberry stomachache the size of Texas. I held my tummy as I walked out to the bus lane, but instead of my bus, I found Mom waiting for me.

"Maggie! Over here!"

I walked slowly, trying to decide how many miles long I should make this guilt trip. Her eyes were filled with apologies. "I'm so sorry, honey. I tried to make it, I really did. And then the dryer broke and I had twenty guests with no clean towels and it was a mess and I am just so sorry."

"It's okay. I guess." I shrugged. "I'll be student of the month at least six more times. Maybe even seven."

She exhaled with relief. "Well, I have to make it up to you. Want to go to the mall?" She must have forgotten whom she was talking to. "No," I said with absolute conviction.

"Want to go to Dairy Queen?"

"Yes," I said with even more absolute conviction.

I ordered my usual Peanut Butter Cup Blizzard and Mom ordered the same, which was weird because I wasn't sure we'd ever have anything in common again. Every time I let myself trust her, she betrayed me. Well, maybe it wasn't as extreme as "betrayal." She wasn't Benedict Arnold or anything. But she did let me down. More than once. And I couldn't forget it. And a Blizzard wouldn't fix it. But maybe two or three Blizzards down the line would. I searched the bottom of my cup for more candy in a silence so cold I got an allover freeze, not just a brain one.

"Maggie, I hope you can forgive me. I know I messed up, but I promise—"

"Promise to never break another promise ever again?"

She looked defeated. "Oh, I can't promise that. I'm not perfect, Maggie. Not even close."

That wasn't what I wanted to hear. "So what do you promise?"

"I promise to try harder." She thought for a second. "And I promise to never—Hey! Are you wearing lip gloss?"

I pulled my lips into my mouth. "No ma'am."

I could tell she didn't believe me but she let me get away with lying for some reason. She hugged me close to her side as we walked toward the car, and I liked that for once, I was the one who couldn't be trusted.

CHAPTER THIRTEEN

Around mid-March the halls at school filled with the glorious smell of rubber cement, the sharp sound of scissors cutting construction paper, and the wonderful buzz of facts being questioned over and over again. It was time for the science fair and it wasn't just any science fair. This was the science fair where I would be defending my blue ribbon.

The year before I'd won top prize for an amazing, no-holds-barred exposé on rain forest destruction. I'd written an extensive report filled with facts and interviews with local tree-hugging hippies. And for my big ta-da, I hadn't done one of those typical, super boring, three-paneled boards everyone else had done. With Mom's help, I'd stapled together over a hundred giant sheets of bulletin board paper and rolled them out across the gym floor. Each piece of paper represented one hundred square miles of rain forest destroyed. It had been a precise dramatization of the crazy amount of rain forest that was chopped down every hour, and it had clinched my victory.

I'd walked away with my head held high triumphantly and I'd even gotten my picture in the paper, which was fun, but ironic because the local paper is probably printed on paper made from rain forest trees. ANYWAY. I'd won, I'd gotten a blue ribbon, and I was going back for another.

Mom and Dad knew the science fair meant A LOT to me and they did whatever they could do to help. Mom excused me from my chores for a couple weeks so I could immerse myself in research and Werther's Originals.[44] And Dad helped me comb through *National Geographics*, even the scary ones with naked tribal people. And their help made Tiffany furious because she had to do her chores and mine for a few weeks, but whatever. I was trying to change the world. The only thing she ever changed was boyfriends.

I usually announced my science fair topic in a big to-do at dinner. Dad would drumroll his fingers on the table and when he stopped, I'd announce my topic and Mom and Dad would *ooh* and *aah* because they're my number-one fans. And you need your number-one fans when you're doing big deal stuff.

~~~~~~~~~~~~~~~~~~~

44. A butterscotch candy that makes you ~~smarter~~ wiser.

But this year, I was keeping my topic a secret. A Top Secret to be revealed when I was too far into research for my parents to make me choose another topic. Which I knew they would do as soon as they found out that I hadn't picked just any of the world's problems to research. I'd chosen a problem that lived in our own house.

This year, I was doing my project on Dad. I was going to get one step closer to fixing him.

When Mom and Tiffany dropped me off at the library, Mom begged me to tell her what I was doing. "Come on, Maggie. A hint?"

I rubbed my hands together like a mad scientist. "In due time, my lady. In due time."

Tiffany rolled her eyes. "You're such a weirdo."

Mom gave her a Mom look. "Knock it off. Maggie, we'll be back after we get your sister a pair of jeans."

"Okay." I reached for my backpack from the backseat and gave Tiffany my most brilliant smile. "Hey Tiffany, know what else you should get at the mall?"

"What?"

"A new face."

Slam! Mom drove away and I high-fived myself for ending on such a zinger.

I opened the library door and the smell of knowledge and dust hit me in the face. I loved everything about the library. I loved the rows and rows of books. I loved the cranky old ladies who read about knitting while knitting. I loved the book alarm that caught book thieves. I loved that while technology progressed, I could still depend on books because no one ever lied in books. And I loved that the librarian loved books just as much as I did and she brought me juice boxes and pretzels when I was studying and I enjoyed them even though you're never supposed to eat or drink in the library but she was in charge and well, the pretzels were sourdough and the juice box was cran-apple. My favorites.

I set up my research lab at my preferred table, next to the A–F American History row. It was the only table in the whole place that didn't wobble and today it was mine. ALL. MINE. I spread out my pencils and my papers and my color-coded index cards. Pink for encyclopedia facts, blue for other reference book facts, and yellow for random thoughts along the way.

I started with the basics: the elusive M encyclopedia. I began at the end and found what I was looking for between Morpheus (the Greek god of dreams) and Mumbai (which is in India, where cows walk around in the streets like they're people).

I had never seen all seventeen letters of Dad's disease in print before:

M-u-l-t-i-p-l-e S-c-l-e-r-o-s-i-s.

They looked like a big deal. I sounded the words out phonetically under my breath so I could understand them fully.

Each letter carried a different weight of its own. The *M* wasn't warm and cozy like a muffin. It was cold and distant like Mars. And the *S* curved like a snake but instead of scales I imagined it was made up of thousands of pins and needles like the ones that pricked and pinched Dad's hands and feet from the inside out. All seventeen letters together felt heavy. Heavier than an elephant. Heavier than a whale shark. Heavier than the biggest meteor in all the universe. It was a heaviness that metaphorically weighed me down from head to toe.

I pushed the encyclopedia away, not wanting the letters to touch me. For the first time I was scared of catching Dad's disease. Because right then I realized I didn't know as much about his disease as I'd thought. In fact, according to the facts, I hardly knew anything. It was time to pull up my bootstraps like I never had before. It was time to get to work.

I filled my pink note cards with one new something after another. Dad's disease was "an inflammatory disease in which the fatty myelin sheaths around the axons of the brain and spinal cord are damaged, leading to demyelization and scarring as well as a broad spectrum of signs and symptoms." I didn't know what any of that meant, but it sounded serious.

Next, I moved on to symptoms. There were so many I decided to highlight the ones Dad had. Symptoms included: tingling, prickling, or numbness in the extremities, muscle weakness or difficulty moving, difficulties with coordination and balance, problems in speech or swallowing, visual problems, fatigue, loss of bladder control, cognitive impairment, intermittent tremors, sensitivity to heat, unstable mood,[45] depression, and paralysis either partial or complete.

I had seen all of these words before, but never all in one place and never specifically related to Dad. My eyes leapt ahead of my brain. I was reading things I didn't understand. I had goose bumps everywhere you get goose bumps.

There was no clear cause. It wasn't a cold. It wasn't something you could catch. The medicines had long names and no one knew if they really worked.[46] The disease evolved over decades and there were two types of it. One kind went away and came back. Another type never went away and only got worse. There were varying degrees of severity with both.

Then I read the last thing in the last paragraph of the entry: There was no known cure.

THERE. WAS. NO. KNOWN. CURE.

A big lump formed in my throat. My eyes filled with water but it wasn't tears. It was sweat from my brain

---

45. He kind of had this. But only when nothing good was on the radio. So I didn't highlight it.

46. Why would anyone invent medicine that didn't work?!

working double time. I closed my eyes and let the brain sweat roll down my face. My brain was learning things my heart didn't want to know. And it was making me mad.

How could my parents keep all of this from me? Did they even know everything that I now knew? Unlikely, since I never saw them do any research. And how could these scientists and doctors be perfectly okay with calling things "unknown" or "inconclusive"? They needed to get with it! Do their jobs! Put on their goggles and not take them off until they'd put together all the pieces of the puzzle! Maybe start with the corner pieces and then work in toward the middle, and if they were missing a piece, they should've looked under the couch.

As soon as I exhausted my mad at them I got even more mad at myself. Why had I never thought about all of this before? I mean, I spent so much time with Dad and most of the time his arms and legs were asleep but I'd never really thought about waking them up. I looked down at my hands. They looked just like his. We even had the same palm lines and knuckle creases. But mine were awake and his were falling asleep. Maybe forever. Why was I just now realizing all of this?

Actually, I'd kind of assumed before that the sleepiness was caused by doing the bad sort of things that I knew Dad had done. Like not doing his homework and dropping out of college and dodging the draft and lying to the neighbors by telling them it was Tiffany blasting the loud music.

I thought it was a kind of punishment that he would eventually pay off. His time-out would end. He would come out of the corner and out of the chair and do good deeds for the rest of his life like save kittens from trees and bald eagles from extinction and we would live happily ever after in a tree house like the Swiss Family Robinson where I would get my own bamboo room and we would look back on the days of when his arms and legs were asleep and say, "Phew. Glad that's over."

But now I knew that it would never be over. Now I knew there was no way to fix Dad.

And then I had a thought that almost made me choke on my Werther's Original. But I made myself stop thinking that thought. There was research to be done and I was going to do it.

I immediately dove into all kinds of scientific books.[47] Before I knew it, I had burned through all but three note cards. I was so lost in research that I didn't even notice Mom standing right next to me.

She tugged on my scarf. "Hey Maggie, ready to go?"

---

47. Most kids only use encyclopedias for their science projects but I've discovered they only give very top-line information. If you sleuth out more specific references, the information gets better and better and you look smarter and smarter.

I quickly made a guard with my arm so she couldn't see my notes and I piled every book into my backpack before she could see the titles. I gripped my note cards in my hands and kept my eyes on the door. All I had to do was make it to the car. Then the coast would be clear. Tiffany would tell me about her jeans and how a size zero is still too big on her and I would respond with some witty yet brilliant remark and Mom would tell us to quit it. But as soon as I walked through the door, the book alarm sounded.

The librarian lady juice-box-giver called me back to the desk and made me open my backpack. There it was: the M encyclopedia.

She shook her head. "Now, you know you can't check out reference materials."

I was mortified. "Yes, ma'am. I'm sorry, it was an accident." Since it was my first offense, she let me off without giving me a book felony or sending me to book jail.

"Aha!" Mom said. "So I know the topic starts with M. Machu Picchu? Um, macaroni and cheese?"

I threw my scarf over my shoulder. "No, Mom. I'll tell you later."

I didn't know when later would actually be. I thought it would be much, much later, like maybe even after I had finished the report. But I just had so many little questions and one big question that couldn't wait. So later turned out to be: dinner.

Everyone was at the table. Mom was in her seat cutting up Dad's chicken. Dad was in his wheelchair waiting to eat. Tiffany and Layla were putting their rolls back in the basket because they ate carbs the day before and they only ate carbs every other day.

And I was pushing my carrots around my plate while Dad asked Layla if she'd finished her English paper. Layla said she hadn't because she still wasn't sure what to write about. Dad told her to just make something up because that's what *he* always did. Mom hit him on the leg even though I now knew he couldn't feel it and told Layla to write something from her heart. Tiffany batted her eyelashes and said, "Write about Bobby, he's in your heart." And then Layla threw a roll at her and then Tiffany threw it back and then I blurted out, "IS DAD GONNA DIE?"

Dad dropped his fork, and not because it slipped. Layla was wide-eyed. Tiffany kicked me under the table. Mom said what I knew she'd say.

"Of course not, honey, why would you ask that?"

I unwrapped my scarf to let my neck breathe. "I'm researching Dad's disease for the science fair. . . . I read some things at the library today."

"Ah, I was afraid that was the *M*," Mom said. "But I was really pulling for macaroni and cheese."

Dad kept his eyes on her as he pushed his chair back from the table. I thought they were going to disappear into the garage like they always did, but he stayed put.

"Who wants a cocktail? I want a cocktail." He pointed at Mom. "Do you want a cocktail?"

Mom stood up. "I would LOVE a cocktail. I'll go fix us cocktails."

Cocktails? REALLY? I didn't want to time travel. I didn't want to hear any stories or learn any lessons or talk about old hippie stuff. I wanted to know what was happening RIGHT NOW.

Tiffany called out to Mom. "I'll take a cocktail."

Layla nodded. "Me too."

I felt myself beginning to cave. I needed something to take the edge off. Sometimes on New Year's Eve, Dad let all of us have a sip of his champagne while Mom wasn't looking. And then Mom would yell from the kitchen, "I can see you." And then we would get the giggles, which I thought meant we were tipsy, but Tiffany said that was impossible from one sip.

I raised my hand. "Make mine a double."

Dad yelled back to Mom. "Honey, the girls want cocktails."

"Okay. Two rum-and-Cokes and three Shirley Temples. Coming right up."

Great. A mock-tail. She better give me two cherries. I needed two cherries.

I let Dad take a sip of his drink and then I made him give it to me straight. "Dad. Are you going to die?"

He took another big gulp. "No. Absolutely not. I'm not going anywhere. Maybe one day when I'm a really old man. But look at me. I'm young and I still have great hair, which means I'm too good looking to die. Everyone knows good looking people don't die."

Okay, fair enough. "Are you going to get sicker?"

Mom took her seat and answered for him. "Not necessarily. Your dad's really strong. Sure, we've had our setbacks, but what do we always do, Maggie?"

Ugh, the family motto? Now? "We pull up our bootstraps."

Mom nodded. "Exactly."

They asked if I had any more questions and I definitely did. I wanted to talk science. How would we find a cure? What could I have invented to help? Was there any truth to the whole "spoonful of sugar" thing from *Mary Poppins*? Because I'd be willing to eat sugar with him if it was true. You know, for moral support.

All this time Layla was super quiet, which wasn't necessarily unusual when Dad and I were dropping science. But when I looked over, tears were pooling her mascara into a black puddle and she was trying to keep it from spilling down her cheeks by staring at the ceiling. When she couldn't hold the dam any longer, she asked if she could be excused and got up from the table without waiting for an answer.

"What's wrong with Layla?" I asked.

"I think it's allergies," Mom said. "You know, the dogwoods are blooming. I'll take her some medicine."

Mom disappeared and then it was just Dad, Tiffany, and me at the table with all the questions.

I was getting out my note cards when Tiffany asked, "So what are all the pills for?" Aha! Maybe I wasn't the only one in the dark.

Dad ran through the pharmacy. "The oblong one keeps me from getting the shakes. The purple and white one keeps my spirits up. And I don't know what the red one does but it looks like one I took out in the desert in the seventies."

GEEZ. I wrinkled my nose. "I don't think you're supposed to tell us that kind of stuff."

He laughed. "I thought we were being honest?"

Mom came out of Layla's room and her eyes were red now too.[48] She took her seat and sipped from her mostly empty glass. "Is there anything else you want to know about, Maggie?" She looked at me with the same look on her face that she had when she broke the news to me about the Easter Bunny.[49]

I hid my note cards. "No ma'am."

"Well, that's all we know, Maggie. That's all anyone knows."

I turned to Dad. "Are you scared?"

He shook his head and puffed up his chest. "Never."

---

48. Someone better do something about all those dogwoods.

49. Just like with Santa—highly suspicious.

I believed him. Then I remembered I had one more question. "Should we be going to church?" I knew God wasn't a doctor and we never learned about him in science class, but maybe we should be covering all our bases. "Should we be praying for a miracle?"

Dad asked Mom for more ice and she disappeared again into the kitchen. "I think God's got his hands full right now, Maggie."

Which was true. All that stuff with the rain forest alone must have been keeping Him pretty busy. But I couldn't let it go. "Maybe we should start going again. Why did we stop?"

Mom returned with Dad's drink, which was full, but not with ice.

He took a sip. "It's just too crowded."

That made sense. Everyone in church was praying for their own miracles, which didn't leave any room for ours. Their prayers were crowding the path to heaven. If we went to church, our prayers would've circled for hours before ever landing. Our prayers needed a lot of room to be heard. We needed to be praying in open fields or in the backyard or at the very least, in our rooms at night.

"Do you pray, Dad?"

Dad looked at me. "Every night."

That night I'm pretty sure we all prayed. I hadn't prayed in a while because honestly I had everything I ever wanted. Good books. Good hair. Great grades. But that night I prayed with all my might. I asked God to save Dad, to cure him, and please for the love of Himself, do something about the dogwoods.

The next morning, Mom and Dad didn't make me pick a new topic. But they did make me promise to ask them questions along the way and let them read the report before I turned it in. We shook on it and I got back to work. After a couple days I was positive I had THE winning project. AGAIN.

For my big ta-da piece, I drew a picture of Dad and diagrammed where everything was happening. I drew arrows where the sleepiness was pulling him this way and that way. Then, with his help, I also put in some cool dude stuff. The arrow next to his eyes said, "Sometimes his eyes are blurry but they will never forget the sight of Jimi Hendrix playing 'The Star Spangled Banner' on his electric guitar which these eyeballs saw in 1969." The arrow next to his brain said, "Sometimes his brain does a lot of tricky things but it will never forget a single word to 'Stairway to Heaven.'"

We finished with a bunch more arrows and facts. I turned my project in and eagerly waited three days for my A.

But on day three, when I got my project back, it was a B.[50] I was DEVASTATED. One catch to the science

----

50. A B!

fair was that only As could be entered, ensuring that only the very best projects competed for the top prize. Getting a B kept me from entering at all. I scrambled to the last page of my report and read Mrs. Hanebury's explanation.

"While I love the personal touches throughout the paper and the extensive research, science fair rules state that you have to propose a solution to your topic's problem, and Maggie, you presented no solution. Next year, pick a problem you can solve."

SERIOUSLY lady? Read the report! There's no cure! What did she want from me? Even scientists couldn't solve this problem!

I stayed after class to challenge the grade, but Mrs. Hanebury wouldn't budge. She insisted she couldn't bend the science fair rules. My blue ribbon dreams were no more.

I went home and told Dad and he was so mad that he asked me to put him in the car and drive him down to the school.

"I can't drive, Dad! I can barely ride a bike!"

"Fine," he said, and we waited for Mom to get home so she could drive us down there where we would raise h-e-double-hockey-sticks. At first I had the fight in me, but then I had to concede, because Mrs. Hanebury was right.

"I don't think there's anything she can do, Dad."

Dad wheeled close to me. "But you worked so hard.

We both did. I've never worked so hard on a school project in my whole life!"

"But I didn't follow the rules. I didn't solve any
problems."

"Well, if that's how you really feel, then okay. But I
still think you deserve to win."

I didn't agree with him. The winner was supposed to
have a clear solution. And all I had were more questions.
The only thing I had confirmed was sometimes you end
up learning things you wish you hadn't. And you can't
unlearn them. I couldn't unknow that there was no cure.
That there was no fixing Dad. I couldn't unthink that
more scary stuff was going to happen. I couldn't unwon-
der if the worst was yet to come.

I could just hope that he was right about one thing:
good looking people don't die.

CHAPTER FOURTEEN

Getting a B on my science fair project really wrecked
me. Not only because Bs were for losers but because
some idiot went on to win MY blue ribbon. Jeremy
Smith did some boring report on windmills and how
they would solve the energy crisis. Yeah right. The only
thing that was going to solve the energy crisis was math
and A LOT of it. The worst part? He didn't even have a
ta-da moment. He just made a lame three-panel board
covered in a bunch of pictures. I just didn't know what
those judges were thinking. Didn't anyone have stan-
dards anymore? You think Albert Einstein ever made a
three-panel board? Of course not! He had awesome hair
and people with awesome hair only did awesome things,
just like Dad and me.

Not only did that terrible B put me in a funk, it put my
GPA in a funk too. I needed to do some major studying

and major extra credit to get it back up to my perfect 4.0. Luckily, spring break was coming up so I had a whole seven days to independently study until my eyeballs fell out.

I asked Mrs. Hanebury if there was anything I could do to get my science grade back on track. She said she'd give me bonus points on the final exam if I grew mold on bread and brought it in for our lesson on penicillin. I gladly accepted the challenge.

When I got home from school on Friday, I commandeered all of the bread from the kitchen. I stashed two loaves under my bed because mold grows in dark places, which I already knew even though I hadn't studied it yet. I pushed both loaves to the farthest, darkest corner, but then I realized it was probably going to smell really bad in a couple days, so I pulled them back out and put them under Tiffany's bed instead. What? She would have done the same thing to me.

And you know what? It totally worked. After a week, my GPA shot back up with the help of the moldiest bread ever. The downside? Tiffany gave me the silent treatment for over a week after she found it growing under her bed. Not that I cared since she never really said anything of interest to me anyway. Did I care about the dance team? No. Did I care about who she was dating? No. Did I care that she got caught sneaking out of the house twice in one week? Sort of, but mostly no. And trust me, the silent treatment was worth it because my grades were better than ever and nothing could bring them down again. Except for one thing.

While it's hard to admit, there was one subject at school I didn't dominate: gym class. It just wasn't my thing. And usually my gym teachers let me get away with not doing too much. And lately it had been especially easy because my teacher was going to have a baby and as she got bigger and bigger we did less and less. One day she even let us read and said we were exercising our eyeballs, which I loved. I probably burned four thousand eyeballs calories that day. She wasn't even due until June which meant it was smooth sailing to the end of the year. That was until she went into labor early and life as I knew it was OVER.

After my gym teacher went on maternity leave, my class joined Coach Eastbrook's class. Coach Eastbrook was the track coach and he ran everywhere including to school. I'm serious, he ran to school every day and every day my bus passed him and every day I thought, "That guy is nuts."

Even more nuts? He made his students run AN ENTIRE MILE. EVERY DAY! I couldn't even walk for two minutes without getting winded. There was no way I was going to deal with this, so I did what any rational human being would do: I lied.

At dinner the night before my first day in his class, I told Mom I wasn't feeling well. She felt my forehead and said I wasn't warm but I swore I was getting sick and that it was probably really serious. To convince her, I did something I never did. I skipped dessert. When she got out the ice cream I politely declined.

"I don't want any."

"Really?!"

"Geez. Don't act so surprised. I just don't feel like it."

"But you never say no to ice cream. Is everything okay?"

"I don't feel good. It's probably the flu. Or mono. Or the plague."

"Well, let's get you to bed. Hopefully, you'll feel better in the morning."

She bought it!

I climbed into bed, which was exactly where I wanted to be because I'd hidden a few[51] Chips Ahoy cookies under my pillow earlier in preparation for skipping dessert.

When I woke up the next morning, Mom had left a note saying I could stay home if I still wasn't feeling well. But I couldn't stay home because I had a feeling there was going to be a pop quiz in science and my pop quiz intuition was never wrong. So I figured I'd go to school, ace the quiz and then check out right before sixth-period gym. It was the perfect plan.

And AHA! There was a pop quiz and I aced it! In between classes I called Mom but she didn't answer

---

51. Seven.

because she was always too busy to answer her phone at work even though I was her daughter and needed her more than anyone else especially at that very moment. So I called Dad, who was deep into Double Jeopardy. I could tell because of how he answered the phone.

"Where is Beirut?"

"Hey Dad, I don't feel good. Can I check out of school?"

"Where is Beijing?"

"Dad! Listen! I need to check out of school!"

"Quick, Maggie, name some other "B" cities!"

"Boise. Belfast. Bangalore."

He finally paid attention. "Those are good. What's up?"

"I need to come home. I am REALLY sick."

"Oh Mags, I'm sorry—"

Yes! I was home free!

"—but I don't think Mom can come get you. Sure you can't tough it out? You only have a couple hours left."

"I have to come home now," I insisted. "I'm too sick to go to gym class."

"Well how about I call your teacher and tell him to let you sit it out until you're feeling better."

Phew. I gave him the school number, thanked him, and gave him Berlin for Final Jeopardy.

I was all smiles as I changed in the bathroom stall with the door locked. My gym clothes were already underneath my school clothes so it didn't take long. And I didn't even put on socks because who needs socks to read? Not me. I found my favorite spot on the bleachers, opened my book to the bookmark, and dug into *A Midsummer Night's Dream.*

I was in the thick of Act II when Coach Eastbrook jogged over. "Hey, Maggie. Why aren't you in formation with the troops?"

What was this? Boot camp? "Didn't you talk to my dad? I'm too sick to run today."

"Yes I did and we agreed a good run is exactly what you need. Do you know endorphins have healing powers?"

I counted on dodging this draft just like Dad. "I can't run. I'll die."

"In twenty years of teaching, no one has ever died on me. Come on," he said with a wave. How was this happening? He led me to the gym door and out onto the track where the rest of my class was stretching.

I put the air brakes on my heels. "I can't, Coach! I conscientiously object!"

He reached for my hand, which I was pretty sure was illegal. "A mile is just four little laps, Maggie."

Four laps! I couldn't run four laps! And then he let out an ungodly whistle and then everyone took off running, including me, because when you see a group of people running, you run too.[52]

~~~~~~~~~~~~~~~~~~

52. It's an evolutionary response.

Every step was instantly excruciating and not just because my lungs were about to explode, but also because I wasn't wearing any socks. In a few minutes I was sure paramedics would be carrying me off the field and they'd be horrified to find my heels completely rubbed raw. I'd live the rest of my life without heels, which meant I would have to tiptoe everywhere, which meant people would think I was reaching for something even when I wasn't. Until the day I died, I'd live as if every single thing was just out of my reach.

I could feel the speed of other kids lapping me once, twice, three times. A whole gaggle of boys finished all four laps before I was halfway through one. I stared at my feet, willing them to go faster, but all they could muster was a chug. A very slow chug. I was just about to give up completely when Mary Winter came jogging across the center of the track toward me.

Great, just what I needed during my darkest half hour. I couldn't believe how perfect she looked. She had just run a mile and looked like she was going to prom. Perfect hair. Perfect ponytail. Perfect smile smiling perfectly. She ran up next to me and then the weirdest thing ever happened. She tried to help me.

"Hey Maggie," she said perfectly. "You don't look so good."

I was so out of breath my brain couldn't pull together a comeback or an insult or even a fact about how I was probably going to die. She jogged in place next to me, which was strange because I thought I was actually making progress but she was moving faster than me and she wasn't going anywhere. She reached back and adjusted her ponytail.

"I talked to Coach and he said I could give you a few pointers."

I tried to run away, but well, I couldn't. I tried ignoring her but she just kept jibberjabbering.

"You're running all hunched over. It's wasting a lot of energy. You need to push your shoulders back. Pretend like there's a triangle on your lower back pulling you up." She pulled my shoulders back and I almost jumped out of my skin. My fight-or-flight reflexes kicked into flight but my legs wouldn't let me so I fought with words instead.

"I know how to run. Every species does."

"Oh. Well, it will be a lot easier if you suck in your diaphragm and breathe through your nose. That's what my dad says anyway. He runs all the time."

I was trapped. So I did what any animal would have done if it was backed up against a wall. I sucked in my diaphragm and breathed through my nose.

Her pointers helped for about five whole seconds and then I couldn't run anymore so I yelled, "I can't run anymore!"

"Don't stop! If you stop, you'll never start again."

I slowed to a snail's pace. "I can't do it ANYMORE."

She ran in front of me, turned around and locked eyes with me, still running. "You can do it, Maggie. I know you can. You just need to stop focusing on the pain."

My thoughts raced ten thousand times faster than my feet. What was this girl talking about? How did she know I could keep going? Why was her ponytail so perfect? (Seriously, not a hair out of place.)

"Come on, match your pace with mine and we'll be done in no time!"

Was this girl JOKING? I wanted to stop, not run faster. I tried to imagine there was a piping-hot glazed donut waiting for me at the finish line, but then I immediately got a cramp in my side. Mary was still jogging backward ahead of me.

"It hurts! I'm stopping."

"Don't stop! Quick! What's your favorite song?"

WHAT! Who would ask a question like that at a time like this?! Was this a slumber party? What was next? Braiding each other's hair? Freezing our underpants? My brain was a blur of confusion and pain.

"The song. About. The states," I gasped.

"I don't think I know that song."

"Yes. You do. The song. In fourth grade. Memorial Day. Spectacular."

"Oh, ha. That one, really? I think I remember it."

I couldn't breathe let alone sing, but Mary sang. And she sang totally off-key, which kind of made me happy. "'Fifty nifty United States from thirteen original colonies'—come on, sing with me!"

Helpless, I joined in, "'Shout 'em, scout 'em, tell all about 'em, one by one till we've given a day to every state, in the USA.'"

We were on our ten thousandth verse when we finally finished lap four. All of the other kids had already gone back to the locker room and were probably dressed and home and watching television with their fathers who hadn't betrayed them.

Coach Eastbrook clicked his stopwatch and yelled, "Twenty-nine minutes and thirty-two seconds! See Maggie, you didn't die."

I collapsed in the grass. "Not yet."

Mary sat down next to me. She reached her hands all the way down to her toes because obviously she didn't have bones.

I rolled my head over in the grass. "You didn't have to do that."

She reperfected her ponytail. "I know. I wanted to." Then she popped up and started jogging in place again. "And don't thank me yet. We have a lot more miles before the end of the semester!" And then she was gone, like a perfect phantom who wore pear-scented body lotion.

I couldn't believe it. I ran a mile without dying. Even more amazing, why did Mary Winter care if I lived or died?

At dinner, I iced my knee because that's what real athletes do. Water dripped on the carpet and Mom yelled, "Maggie, what are you doing?"

I pressed another cube of ice to my other knee. "I'm icing my knees. I ran a mile today."

"You're supposed to put the ice in a bag. Duh." Tiffany sighed. "You're such a dork."

I was just about to throw the half-melted ice cube at her when Mom interrupted.

"You ran a whole mile today? I thought you didn't feel good."

"Well, my throat is still sore." I coughed a little. "But I pushed through it."

"Like father, like daughter," Dad said. "What was your time?"

"Twenty minutes. Give or take nine minutes."

Tiffany laughed. "Slugs run faster than that!"

I'd had enough of her so I ran[53] to my room and slammed the door much harder than a slug ever could.

For some reason she followed me.

"Get out of my room!" I yelled.

~~~~~~~~~~~~~~~~~
53. Yes, I run now.

"This is my room too!" she yelled back.

"Why are you such a jerk?"

"Why are you such a dork? Calm down."

I threw my pillow and just missed her head. It wasn't an accident. It was a warning shot.

"Hey! It's not my fault you're a disgrace to our entire family!"

I threw another pillow and didn't miss. "Oh, like you are every Friday night?"

She lunged at me. I lunged at her.

Mom rushed in and pulled us apart. "What is going on in here?"

We both pointed at each other. "She started it!" we yelled at the same time.

Dad rolled into the room. Or he rolled in as far as he could without rolling into the sea of dirty clothes. "I don't care who did what or who told on who. All I am going to say is, Maggie, I cannot believe you ran a mile."

Mom hit him on the arm to remind him we were in trouble.

Dad laughed. "I'm serious. I've never even seen her walk fast."

"You're one to talk," I said under my breath.

Mom gave me a look. "Hey, what's the house rule?"

"You're the only one allowed to make fun of Dad," I recited.

Mom crossed her arms. "And don't you forget it."

"Can I go now?" Tiffany huffed.

"No." Mom wheeled Dad away and turned around. "No one is leaving until someone says she's sorry." And then she shut the door.

I crawled into bed and mummified myself in my blanket. Tiffany came over and shoved me. I didn't move a muscle. She shoved me again.

"Just apologize so we can leave."

I ripped the blanket off. "Apologize to you? You're the one ruining my life!"

"Whatever. I don't even believe you ran that far anyway."

"Well, you can ask Mary Winter because she ran with me!"

"Mary Winter? Bo's sister? Isn't she, like, popular?"

"Yeah, so what?"

"So why would she talk to *you*?"

"I don't know, why does her brother swap spit with *you*?"

"Hey! That's none of your business."

"Then stop making it my business!"

She stormed out of the room and I yelled after her. "APOLOGY ACCEPTED!"

Two days later in gym class, I secured three layers of Band-Aids on my heels and carefully positioned my socks. And then I put on another pair of socks just in case. I walked out of the locker room, through the gym, and onto the track, certain I was going to have to go it alone today. No way would Mary Winter want to help me two classes in a row.

But she did.

"Hey Maggie, what are we singing today?"

I shook my head. "It's okay. You don't have to run with me anymore."

She leaned down to tighten her laces. "Why not?"

I leaned down and tightened my laces too, because it looked professional. And then I thought, since I was down here, I might as well pull up my bootstraps too.

"Because this is my fight, Mary. Not yours." I patted her on the shoulder, saluted, and took my place on the track. I had to prove to myself that I could do it. I gazed around the track and visualized it as a Scantron that I was about to fill in with every right answer. My feet would be my number two pencil.

I reached for my toes one last time and then another pair of feet joined mine. And they belonged to Mary Winter.

"Hey, I get it if you don't want to run together. But maybe after class you can talk me through our science homework? I'm lost."

My mind wanted to tell her to go away. But my feet, legs, and spleen[54] remembered the pain of trying to run by myself. Maybe it was okay to need someone's help. Just this once.

~~~~~~~~~~~~~~

54. Whatever a spleen is.

I scooted over and made room for her next to me on the track. "We can talk about it while we run. I have it memorized."

So we ran and we sang and I almost died once and then I recovered and then I dropped some knowledge about mitochondria and then I almost threw up and then I got a cramp and then I remembered the triangle on my lower back and then we only had three more laps to go.

And I realized that maybe Mary Winter wasn't out to get me. Maybe she wasn't even being mean with the flower back in February. Maybe she wasn't trying to ruin my life. Maybe she was just nice. Maybe it was okay if Clyde liked her.[55]

Maybe we were friends.

---

55. Just as long as she NEVER ever liked him back.

CHAPTER FIFTEEN

I must've gained a lot of muscle from running because I no longer needed Mom's help getting the Nutella jar open, which meant I got Nutella without her permission, which meant my life was complete. And I felt better than ever when school ended. I got all As again and won every award at Awards Night. Again.

I kept my chin and bootstraps up as I signed Mary's yearbook at the Yearbook Signing Party after Study Hall. She'd blocked off a little corner just for me and I wrote extra small so I could fit in all my well wishes for her over the summer. I wrote how lucky it was that she got to go to summer school![56] And how double lucky it was that we became friends in gym class and I hoped we would have a class together again next year, but

---

56. I tried to get into summer school with Mary. But my advisor says it's for kids who are behind, not ahead. Their loss.

maybe not gym. Maybe something super fun like Latin or geometry. And I promised to keep running or at the very least take up speed walking like the old ladies in the mall with the cool hats and even cooler fanny packs.

I was just dotting my last i when another yearbook slid across the table next to me. I looked up and there he was: Clyde.

"Hey Maggie, wanna sign my yearbook?"

I almost choked. And I wasn't even chewing anything. Which was unusual.

I was nervous but I pulled it together. "Um yeah, sure." I opened his yearbook and it was covered in like a zillion signatures mostly from girls. I couldn't find an empty spot anywhere. He seemed to have gotten really popular. Especially with the ladies.

"Where should I sign?"

"Hmmm." He scratched the back of his head like some kind of rock star philosopher. "How about next to your picture?"

I turned to the page where my picture should have been. "Oh, I don't have one this year. See?"

"Were you sick on picture day or something?"

"No, I wanted to wear a tricorn hat like George Washington and they wouldn't photograph me wearing it. So I refused to have my picture taken at all."

"Really?" Clyde laughed. "That's pretty cool. Standing up for what you believe in and everything."

"Well, I was sitting. But thanks." I found an empty space on the second to last page. "How about right here?"

"Perfect. Want me to sign yours?"

I couldn't believe it. He wanted to sign my yearbook. I tried to keep my hand from shaking as I passed it to him.

He opened it and was immediately impressed. "Wow, there are a lot of signatures in here. From teachers."

I tried to be modest. "Yeah, they *really* like me."

He started writing and my brain blanked. What should I write? Should I tell him to keep in touch? No. You can't keep in touch if you're not in touch in the first place. Should I profess my love for him in a no-holds-barred essay referencing my extensive research about how we were MEANT2B? Maybe not.

What would Dad tell me to write? He would tell me to say something cool. So I did just that:

Dear Clyde,
Have a perfect summer. I'll see you next year close to the harvest! Get it? Like Neil Young's Harvest? I hope you got it. I'm sure you did. You get everything. And if you need any book recommendations for over the summer, I have about a thousand.
Sincerely,[57]
Maggie

---

57. Love. God, I wanted to write LOVE.

I handed the yearbook back to him and he handed mine back to me and away he went, off into the metaphorical summer sunset. I wasn't by his side, but I hoped I was in his heart.

As soon as he disappeared around the corner, I searched for the page he signed in my yearbook. I couldn't find his signature anywhere. I went page by page and finally found it where I least expected it. On the same page in the same square where my picture was supposed to be, Clyde had sketched a portrait of me. And I was wearing a tricorn hat just like George Washington's. Next to it he had written, "Stay cool Maggie Mayfield. Peace. Clyde."

I pressed the book close, hoping his words would transfer by osmosis directly into my heart. He thought I was cool! The final bell of the school year rang and I realized I had never ever been happier.

I decided I would keep up with my running over the summer. Well, for a couple weeks anyway. I ran up and down our neighborhood and saw things I'd never seen before because I'd really only been up our street in a car. The farthest I'd ever walked was to the mailbox and that was only once a month when *National Geographic* arrived.

It turned out there was a whole world out there full of other families doing other things. I passed one house with a dad playing basketball with his son and I wondered if Dad's legs were awake and if I were a boy, would we being doing the same thing? Probably not. I bet even as a boy I would be too smart for sports.

I'd always stop in front of the house at the top of the hill when I was on an evening run. I'd peer into the window where the mom was always in the kitchen doing dishes or making dinner or cleaning something. And I'd remember when my mom was always doing something in our kitchen window and it seemed like forever ago. Before she was a puddle of clothes. Before I had to share her with all those hotel guests. So much had changed since the summer before. And not just my calves, although they were significantly shapelier.

I even hung out with Layla and Tiffany and not against my will. When they lathered up in SPF 0 and lay out on towels in the driveway, I joined them. Well, I joined them from the safety of the shade I'd created with three umbrellas and an old tarp from the garage. I didn't want to damage my fair skin. Dad always said I would have been adored in the Victorian era. Which I liked to think about because I always felt like I belonged to every era except the one I was born into. I especially felt a connection to eras where they wore layers and layers of underpants and read books by candlelight while enjoying madeleines and drinking tea.

It was shaping up to be a perfect summer. Until one day when it took a sudden and peculiar turn.

I was partaking in some light summer reading of *Leaves of Grass* while Layla and Tiffany read *Seventeen* magazines in their usual sunning spot. All was quiet on the home front. Even Dad was outside with us catching some rays while reading *Zen and the Art of Motorcycle Maintenance* for the millionth time.

But the quiet was broken when Mom's car zoomed up the driveway. She slammed on the brakes and just stopped short of pancaking Layla and Tiffany. They jumped up in terror, Dad yelled some bad words, and Mom freaked.

"What are you doing lying in the middle of the driveway?!" she screamed out the window.

"Us?!" Tiffany yelled. "What are you doing going ninety up the driveway?! In the middle of the afternoon?!"

"Everyone calm down," Dad commanded. And then he laughed. "And let's remember it was your mother who almost killed you. Not me."

"That's enough. I really am sorry," she said. "I should have called first to tell you I was coming home early. But I have good news. Phyllis and Donny are coming to visit!"

Oh dear. Phyllis and Donny were Mom and Dad's hippie burnout friends from way back. They used to visit when I was little whenever they were on their hippie motorcycle trips to hippie places across the country. But we hadn't seen them in a while. I assumed they'd been kidnapped or had turned to a life of crime. This was exactly what my perfect summer didn't need: a night of swapping antiwar stories with a bunch of degenerates.

Mom rushed us all inside. "Time to clean up. They'll be here tomorrow."

"Tomorrow?" I asked. That didn't seem like enough time to hide the valuables. "What's the rush?"

"Well, it's your dad's and my wedding anniversary. What better way to celebrate than with friends? Plus, we need witnesses."

"Witnesses to what?! Are you planning a bank heist?!"

Dad laughed, which I thought was the wrong reaction for someone being accused of a felony. "Your mother and I are going to renew our wedding vows right here."

"What's that mean?"

Mom smiled. "It means there's going to be a wedding."

The next morning I heard a loud rumble from the window. Two homeless-looking people were parking their motorcycle in our driveway. Dad joined me at the window and waved to them.

"Don't wave at them!" I yelped. "For all we know, they could be murderers!"

"I'm afraid we have to let these murderers inside."

I leaned forward. They looked like they had done time. Hard time. I had to get Tiffany. If anyone knew how to chase off bad people, it was Tiffany. She chased me away all the time and I was a good person.

I ran to our room and flung open the curtains. "Look outside!" I hissed at Tiffany, who was still prone on the bed. "Are these the scariest people you've ever seen?"

"No, you're the scariest person I've ever seen," she said without even looking.

Layla must have heard the panic in my voice because she came to see what was up.

"Do you think they're going to kill us in our sleep?" I asked.

"No, but they are creepier than I remember. They even have skeletons on their shirts. What's creepier than that?"

That made me wonder where else they were keeping skeletons.

Layla looked worried. "God, I hope they don't come to *my* wedding one day." She had a point.

"Geez, I hope they don't come to mine either."

Tiffany was awake now. "No one is coming to your wedding, Maggie. Not even the groom."

She was the worst. But I didn't have time to deal with her. I ran into the living room. "Hey parents. We have a consensus. These people are terrifying and we don't really think you should let them in."

There was a knock at the door.

"Too late." Mom laughed.

"I can't die! I'm going to be president! Of the United States! Of America!"

Dad shushed me away while Mom opened the door.

Phyllis was the first one in. "Hey y'all!"

As her skull shirt moved closer, I started to lose it. We were all gonna die. I'd never be president. Forget of the United States, I'd never be president of my class and I had a really good platform for the next election too: free pizza Fridays! But I'd never get to rally for it because I'd be dead. With no free pizza for anyone ever again.

Phyllis hugged Mom so hard I thought Mom's arms might pop off. "I've missed you so much," her scratchy voice kept repeating.

When she finally released Mom, I got a good look at her. The first thing I noticed was the mood ring she wore as a wedding band. It was bright red, which meant she was happy/excited/anxious and/or in love. The next thing I noticed was her long wavy red hair, followed by her blue jeans that belled at the bottom. And then I noticed the skeletons on her shirt again. And then I noticed they were heading straight for me and then I took a deep breath.

My feet left the ground as she pulled me into the skull on her chest, which I assumed wasn't the last skull I would see that day.

"Oh my gawd! You look just like your daddy!"[58]

My feet thumped back to the ground and Phyllis

58. I know lady, keep reminding me.

moved on to her next victims, Layla and Tiffany.

"Look at these beauties! Y'all look just like your mother! She was such a little knockout."

Dad wheeled around next to Phyllis. "She's still a knockout."

Phyllis's mood ring faded to green, which meant she was uneasy/restless/scared. I wondered why she felt any of those things. Maybe she didn't recognize Dad without long hair? Maybe she was scared the police had bugged him with a wiretap? Maybe she'd never seen a wheelchair with an "I'm proud of my Honor Roll student" bumper sticker stuck to the back of the seat?[59]

She took a deep breath and tears welled in her eyes, turning her blue mascara into an ocean.

"Is that my Danny?"

Dad wheeled closer and pinched her tush.

"Yep, that's my Danny!" she yelped. "What do you say? Are you ready to get hitched? Again?!"

Donny came in next and he didn't say much but he high-fived all of us, which was totally weird. He put their bags on the floor and they immediately made our whole house smell like the Renaissance festival. I snooped around their stuff and took in every detail just in case I needed to explain anything to the police.

~~~~~~~~~~~~~~~~~~

59. I put this bumper sticker on Dad's wheelchair. He doesn't know it's there.

Donny set a banjo against the wall and Phyllis pulled something wrapped in a scarf out of her bag. It might have been a gun, so I closed my eyes and mentally prepared for the end. But nothing happened, and when I opened my eyes she was holding out a giant egg with a painting on it.

"This is for your daddy. He always wanted me to paint him a wolf howling at the moon."

"Did you make this?"

"I sure did. It's one of my babies."

I mumbled "cool," but I nervously wondered if this woman laid eggs. Sure, scientifically, physically, and anatomically it wasn't possible, but you never knew, especially with this weirdo. I would have asked Dad, but he probably wouldn't have told me for another ten years.

Donny fixed the grown-ups Coca-Colas with more than Coca-Cola in them. Dad told us to clean up outside for the ceremony, so Layla, Tiffany, and I wandered into the backyard.

I still didn't really get what was happening. I mean they were already married. They didn't need to get married again. That's like taking a test twice, although I wasn't opposed to taking tests twice.

I picked up some sticks and pinecones and threw them over the fence. I'd forgotten how big our backyard was. Great, even more places to hide a body. I pulled a few weeds and then I heard everyone come outside.

Dad was looking at Donny's motorcycle all wide-eyed.

"What do you say, Danny?" Donny asked with a nudge. "How about a ride?"

Tiffany's extra-bad-kid side kicked in. "Yes, Dad! Do it!"

"Saddle me up!" Dad shouted.

I was clearly the only sane person in the family. "No way!" I protested. "You could crash and break a femur, tibia, fibula, patella, or any of the other two hundred and six bones."

"Let's just make sure my face is okay. I like my face." Dad winked at me.

Donny handed him a helmet and laughed. "In that case, you'll be needing this."

I really didn't want him to go. I grabbed Mom's hand in solidarity but she dropped it so she could position Dad's chair right next to the motorcycle while Donny took his place behind the handlebars. The whole thing was terrifying, so I tried to hold Tiffany's hand out of desperation but she shook her hand away because she's the meanest girl alive. And then out of nowhere Phyllis grabbed my hand and held it tightly and for the first time all day, I didn't feel like I was going to get murdered.

Mom counted to three and hoisted Dad up onto the motorcycle seat. He pulled his sleeping legs on either side of the motorcycle and wrapped his arms around Donny's waist. Phyllis let go of my hand and wound bungee cords around Dad and Donny until they were one body with four arms and two heads. And then Donny stepped on a pedal and then a big engine roared and then Dad yelled some curse words and Mom shouted, "Bring him back in one piece please! We're getting married tomorrow!"

Dad threw a peace sign as they took off down the road toward only God knows where.

While they were gone, I beat Layla at UNO, Phyllis French braided Tiffany's hair, and Mom held her breath staring out the window. Finally a headlight bounced off the wall. We ran outside and watched Dad, Donny, and the motorcycle purr into the driveway.

As soon as Dad was unbungeed from Donny, he collapsed into Mom's arms. She had to set him up in his chair because he was all dangly like a rag doll. I don't know where they'd gone but Dad smelled like trees and sweat and fireflies and rock 'n' roll if rock 'n' roll had a smell.

He lifted up his shirt. "See how tough these marks from the bungee cords make me look?"

Phyllis cranked up the stereo so I had to yell over the music. "Oh man, does it hurt?" But Dad didn't hear me. All anyone could hear was some lady screaming something about buying her a Mercedes-Benz.

We ate dinner and Mom rushed us off to bed without dessert, which wasn't cool because dessert was the only reason I ate dinner. Tiffany and I got into our beds while Layla slid into the sleeping bag on the floor and Mom quickly wished us good night, turned out the lights, and shut the door. Geez, she could have at least pretended like she cared about us.

The next morning, the most amazing smell in all the land woke up my nose and carried my whole body into the kitchen. Could it be? Certainly it wasn't peach pie baking. Not so early. But I peered into the oven and sure enough, it was there, the most perfect peach pie bubbling over.

"Smells amazing, right?"

"YES," I answered without breaking my gaze with the perfect pie.

"I think she's about ready. Let's get her out."

It was only then that I realized I had been talking to Phyllis, not Mom. She must have been making it for the wedding.

Defeat settled on my shoulders. "It looks amazing. It will be hard to wait for it."

"Don't be silly, little one! This pie is for breakfast!"

PIE FOR BREAKFAST! Maybe she wasn't a murderer. Maybe she was the most amazing woman ever!

Phyllis grabbed a potholder and opened the oven door. My nose followed the pie all the way to the counter.

"Can we eat it right now?"

"Let's wait for it to cool a little. I'll get the ice cream."

Pie AND ice cream FOR BREAKFAST? I ran down the hall and woke up my sisters.

"Eyes open, ladies! We're having pie AND ice cream for breakfast!"

They moaned and groaned and didn't move an inch. Whatever. Their loss. I knocked on Mom and Dad's door.

"Parents! Wake up! There's pie FOR BREAKFAST!"

I didn't hear a peep. What was wrong with these people? I had the human decency to share probably the greatest news we were ever going to get as a family and they couldn't have cared less. But I didn't have time to dwell on their nonsense, I had pie to eat.[60]

I was already on my second slice when the Mayfield family finally joined my new best friends Phyllis and Donny at the table. Dad looked like he'd been hit by a truck. And he smelled weird. So I said, "You smell weird."

"Well, you look weird."

"Hey! You're not allowed to say stuff like that. You're my dad!"

He clutched his forehead. "I'm sorry. I'm sorry. I just have the worst headache."

Mom handed him some aspirin and a slice of pie. "This should help. I see you've made a couple of friends, Maggie."

"Oh we're big fans." Phyllis smiled.

"She already lobbied me for my vote and everything," Donny said.

---

60. For breakfast!

"It's important to get to know your constituents," I explained.

Mom took a piece of pie too, which was very un-Mom-like. "Well, I expect to see all of you on the dance floor later."

I still didn't get it. "Why do you have to renew your wedding vows anyway? Did they expire?"

"No, no. It's just a nice thing to do," Mom said.

"It's a nice way of reminding your mother she's stuck with me," Dad added. "Forever."

Mom disappeared down the hall and came back with two fancy dresses I'd never seen before. "Here you go," she told Layla and Tiffany. "You're going to be my bridesmaids."

They *oohed* and *aahed* and disappeared into the bathroom to try them on.

Dad wheeled next to me and handed me a bow tie. "And you're going to be my best man, Maggie."

"I am not a boy! First you say I look weird and then you think I'm a boy?! What is wrong with you people?!"

"Sorry! Sorry! I didn't mean best man. I meant best daughter. Will you be my best daughter?"

"I hate bows, you know," I said as I grudgingly took the tie.

"What's wrong with bows?"

Mom answered before I could. "*Everything*."[61]

---

61. Exactly.

The wedding wasn't a big to-do or anything. We weren't even going to a church. We stayed at our house. Dad had hired someone to come do the ceremony. I thought that would mean a priest. But Dad had hired an Elvis impersonator who just happened to also be an ordained minister.

Layla, Tiffany, and Mom were taking forever in the bathroom getting ready and Phyllis and Donny had borrowed the car to pick up the cake at the bakery. So Dad and I watched the news while we waited in our ties.

I shook my head. "Can you believe this oil crisis?"

"Are you sure you're only eleven?"

"I know. I can't believe it either."

Layla and Tiffany emerged from the bathroom in their fancy new dresses humming "Here Comes the Bride" and Mom emerged with a big *ta-da* in the most beautiful white dress with her most beautiful red hair swept around her most beautiful freckled face.

Dad whistled and I ran to hug her.

"You look like frosting."

"Thank you. I think," Mom laughed.

Tiffany pried me away. "Don't lick her."

Phyllis and Donny arrived with the cake at the same time as a pink Cadillac pulled into the driveway. It was my duty as best daughter to escort pretend Elvis to the backyard where he was to marry Mom and Dad under a big oak tree we'd decorated with crepe paper bells. Then

I took my place next to Dad with Mom and Dad's rings, which were still warm from their hands.

When Elvis pushed Play on the boom box, Layla walked down the aisle, followed by Tiffany, and then Mom appeared, escorted by Phyllis and Donny. We all gathered around them and Dad grabbed Mom's hand and Mom leaned over and kissed him even though you're not supposed to do that until the pretend Elvis pronounces you man and wife but I guess it was okay since they were already man and wife.

The pretend Elvis began, "Do you take this man to be your husband, for better or worse, richer or poorer, in sickness and in health, and do you promise to make him your only hunka hunka burning love forever?"

Mom laughed. "I do."

Pretend Elvis kneeled next to Dad's chair. "Do you take this woman to be your wife, for better or worse, richer or poorer, in sickness and in health, and do you promise to make her your earth angel from here to eternity?

"Of course." Dad's voice cracked. He was taking this really seriously. "I do."

I gave them their rings and then some other stuff happened that included more kissing and then there was CAKE! From my favorite bakery! The cake had a tiny man and woman on top that you couldn't eat which I knew because I tried and almost lost a tooth.

But I recovered and ate more cake while Layla and Tiffany talked about their weddings and how they would be huge and spectacular and rich and I could see Dad doing math in his head.

I was carefully constructing the perfect bite of cake that was 90% frosting and 10% cake when I asked, "Was your first wedding as cool as this one?"

Mom took the rest of the cake away because she knew when to cut me off. "Our first wedding was great. Your father wore a white tux and platform shoes because he is ridiculous. And a friend made my dress and we danced to Gladys Knight and Eric Clapton and then your father's friends wrote something in shaving cream on our car that they shouldn't have."

I scraped the last microscopic piece of frosting from my plate. "What did they write?"

Dad shook the ice in his glass and opened his mouth but I interrupted.

"I know, I know. You'll tell me in ten years."

Layla pushed the rest of her cake toward me. "What do you remember, Dad?"

Dad took the last sip from his glass and time traveled. "I remember your mother looking like a knockout. Just beautiful. And I remember a lot of dancing and shaking a lot of hands and smiling so hard my face hurt and I remember the punch. And then I don't remember much after the punch."

I turned to Phyllis and Donny. "What do you guys remember?"

Phyllis laughed. "Not much more than your dad."

Donny said, "We had the punch too."

"Well, I'll always remember this wedding," I vowed. "And this cake."

"Oh well, it's not over yet, sweetie. Don't you know what happens next?" Mom asked.

"More cake?!" I hoped.

"Even better." Mom beamed. "A honeymoon."

CHAPTER SIXTEEN

The best thing about Mom and Dad's honeymoon was that it wasn't just for Mom and Dad. They were taking us along too! And we were going to the beach! In Florida! We said our good-byes to Phyllis and Donny and a few days later the house was abuzz with the busyness of packing.

I shoved my swimsuit and fifteen books into my suitcase and I was Florida-ready. We left extra early in the morning so Dad would have time to hang with his friends at the airport before we took off. I checked one bag and Mom checked the food bag, her bag, and Dad's bag and then Layla and Tiffany checked their entire wardrobes. I didn't understand why their suitcases were so big when their clothes were so small, but whatever.

We said a million hellos to a million people and I was told I looked "just like Dad" a million times, which was really starting to bother me. I didn't have a mustache!

I didn't have glasses! I wasn't a dude! I was a girl and everyone needed to just deal with it! Anyway, we finally got on the plane and buckled up and an hour and fifteen packs of pretzels later, we landed in Orlando.

A shuttle took us to our hotel, where my sisters immediately changed into their teeny swimsuits and headed for the pool. Mom lathered me up in SPF 9000 and then I put on a giant shirt, picked up a book, and looked for the biggest umbrella I could find.

Mom and Dad took longer to get ready because it took Mom forever to cover Dad in sunblock because he was 90% hair. But they eventually came down and Mom waved my sisters and me over.

"I'm going to buy a float and we're going to pull your dad to the water on it, okay?"

That sounded crazy so I said, "That sounds crazy."

"There's no other way," she said. "We can't carry him all the way down there."

I looked at my calves. "I dunno. I've been working out and I really think we can."

She laughed. "I'll be back with a float. Watch your father!"

We looked over at Dad, who smiled and waved as he sipped on a drink with a tiny umbrella in it. Oh dear.

Mom came back a little while later with the float and we all took turns blowing it up. Once we got the last cubic inch of air in, we wheeled Dad next to the stairs that led to the beach.

"Okay, here's the plan," Layla said. "Mom and I are going to lift Dad onto the float. And then Maggie, you grab the corner by his left foot. Tiffany, you grab the corner by his right foot, and Mom and I will pull from the middle."

"What should I do?" Dad asked.

"Try not to fall off," Mom said.

Mom and Layla gathered all their strength to pick up Dad and position him on the float. Then we all took our places.

"Is everybody ready?" Layla asked.

"I've never been more ready," Dad said.

On a count of three, we were off. We yanked the float across the sand with all our might as Dad sang "Good Vibrations." Just when I thought my arms would fall off, we reached the water. Tiffany rummaged in her bag and brought out a mask and snorkel. "Can you still do this?"

"Of course I can," Dad declared. "I am one with the sea."

She strapped the mask and the snorkel to his head and we floated him out to the water, then turned him onto his tummy so he could put his face in the water while his legs dangled over the sides. Off he went, searching the sea for fish and other terrifying things. Layla stayed with him to keep him company.

As we walked out of the water, Mom looked at Tiffany. "Why don't you stay with Dad too. Okay?"

"But I want to work on my tan," Tiffany huffed.

"You can work on it later. I promise."

Tiffany finally stopped whining and joined Layla and Dad while Mom and I walked back up the beach.

"Why didn't you want me to stay with Dad?" I asked. "I would have."

"Because I only want to worry about one person drowning at a time," Mom said.

"Good point."

We staked out a spot with a giant umbrella and opened our giant books and started our honeymoon.

A little while and a hundred pages later, Mom decided it was time to go in, so we walked down the beach to get Dad. He was tan and sticky and he couldn't move a muscle, even more than usual. The heat had really done a number on him and his legs wouldn't bend and his arms wouldn't straighten but eventually we got him stable enough on the float to drag him back up the beach. We pulled and pulled and I think he gained a thousand pounds in the ocean. But it didn't seem to bother him since he was having a great time telling everyone on the beach that he was really rich and that we were his servants. Finally we got him back into his chair and Mom wheeled him to the room while I got our things and Layla and Tiffany stayed to soak up the last hour of sunlight.

After the sun set, Mom began making us peanut butter and jelly sandwiches from the food suitcase while Tiffany made herself a fort on the floor.

"I don't know why I have to sleep on the floor. It isn't fair."

Mom handed her a sandwich. "Well, there are only two beds and Layla is your dad's favorite and Maggie is mine."

"Thanks a lot!"

"Calm down. I was just kidding."[62]

Tiffany finally stopped pouting when Dad said we could order a movie off the TV. We all ate and showered and snuggled into our places to watch a PG-13 movie because I wouldn't watch an R-rated movie because I refused to break the law.

The rest of the honeymoon was mostly the same: sun-blocking, dragging Dad down the beach, reading under umbrellas, and then dragging Dad back up the beach. On the very last morning, we woke up before the sun and flew home.

All our dirty clothes from the trip made the biggest pile of laundry in the world. I promised Mom I'd separate the whites from the darks as soon as I unpacked my books, which I knew would take forever and hopefully by the time forever was over someone else would have done it. At least that was my plan.

I emptied my backpack and was lining up Emily Dickinson next to William Shakespeare when I saw there was something in Mark Twain's place on my bookshelf. It was the little man and the little woman from the top of Mom and Dad's wedding cake.

---

62. She wasn't kidding.

Aha! In my cake coma, I'd forgotten that I'd set them there to watch over the rest of my books while we were away. I grabbed the tiny statues and ran into Mom and Dad's room to show them, but I was stopped by the smell of sick. Dad was throwing up and Mom was holding the bathroom trash can under his chin.

"Is Dad okay?"

He threw up again and Mom shooed me away. "Yes, he's fine. Go, Maggie. I'm taking care of it."

I walked out slowly just in case she needed me, but she didn't ask for my help.

I set the tiny man and tiny woman on their dresser. They looked like they belonged together. I was halfway out the door when I heard something fall.

I turned around. The tiny man was on the ground.

Mom picked him up and then she shut the door.

CHAPTER SEVENTEEN

Mom said Dad had caught a bug while we were traveling which was weird because the rest of us were fine. And if anyone was going to get sick, it should've been me because I had run out of Flintstones vitamins a month ago and Mom still hadn't restocked my supply. But for some reason, this sick bug only wanted Dad so for two whole weeks, he slept and ate saltines and slept some more. Finally on the last day of June he started feeling like a cool dude again, which was perfect timing because the Fifteen Days of Fun were only a day away.

Every year, my birthday was rudely interrupted by something. Like Dad's company picnic, which had happened on my tenth birthday. Or Layla's dance camp recital that had happened on my ninth birthday. Or Dad's first day of not working and subsequent time traveling that had happened on my last birthday. So I decided my birthday needed more than one day to be celebrated. It needed fifteen.

Thus, the Fifteen Days of Fun were born. My birthday is July 15th, so celebrating every day of the two weeks leading up to it would make up for any potential disasters on the actual day. Mom and Dad were on board with my plan and they forced Layla and Tiffany on board too, which I didn't mind because, whatever, I was getting fifteen birthdays.

On July 1st, we had a kickoff dinner of my choosing and I chose traditional American fare since I was a traditional American. Since Dad still wasn't feeling 100%, I got to eat half his hamburger. And his potato salad. And his baked beans. And his ice cream. And then I went on an after-dinner run with Tiffany that turned into a walk because we were both so full we could have died.

On July 2nd and 3rd, Mom took me on a two-day library marathon where I checked out so many books I had to let my book bag straps out all the way. And then on July 4th, we went downtown to see the fireworks and Dad came along, making it his first trip out of the house since vacation. We had a great time watching the big sparkly fireworks and the little sparkly fireworks and the ones that twisted and the ones that dangled and then Dad sang "Proud to Be an American" at the top of his lungs because he liked to humiliate us in public.

On week two, even though Dad still wasn't all the way better, he took me to the movies. We saw an R-rated one even though I protested and halfway through it, bad guys flashed on the screen and Dad covered my eyes with his hand. He made me swear I wouldn't tell Mom, but of course I did and then Dad got in big trouble, but not really.

The next day, Layla let me ride in Bobby's TRUCK and we PEELED OUT of the driveway and listened to the radio really LOUD and they took me to DAIRY QUEEN and I got a BLIZZARD. Even Tiffany tried to contribute to the fun by letting me have the room to myself for a whole night. That was foiled when Mom found out she wasn't really spending the night where she said she was spending the night. But watching her get in trouble was still a ton of fun.

And then suddenly it was the day before my birthday and Mom surprised me with an early present. She pushed an envelope across the dinner table.

"Open it."

I tore through the flap and found a flyer. "What's this?"

Mom beamed. "There's a day camp for writers tomorrow at the library and I thought you'd like to go. Great presidents have to be great writers too, right?"

Writing camp! Why hadn't I known this kind of amazing thing existed?! I gave her a hug. "Thanks, Mom! This is awesome!"

Tiffany made a face and snorted. "Nerd alert."

"Careful, Tiffany," Dad warned. "You don't want your face to freeze that way for all eternity."

I didn't care what she thought. I stared at the flyer. "My first camp for grown-ups. This is perfect." I didn't do regular camp. I just wasn't an egg-toss-tug-of-war-water-balloon-fight kind of girl. I was more of a sharpened-pencils-deep-thoughts-spill-your-guts kind of girl, and I was glad Mom realized that.

That night, I laid out my best overalls with my best T-shirt and my new Chuck Taylors that I'd gotten on the seventh day of fun. The only thing missing was my favorite scarf. I searched high and low and even sideways under Tiffany's bed, but I couldn't find it. Writers need their rest, so I packed my book bag and decided the scarf would have to wait until morning.

I woke up with an official twelve-year-old stretch. I'd let myself sleep in a little later than usual because I wanted to have enough energy for what was sure to be the best birthday ever. The fourteen days leading up to it had been the bee's knees and today wasn't going to be any different. I just needed to find my scarf and then it was off to a full day of writing and feeling and emoting, which may all have been the same thing, but I wasn't sure.

I made my debut from the hallway with a big "good morning, family!" But my family didn't seem excited to see me. Tiffany was on the phone while Mom was pulling burnt muffins from the oven. And Dad and Layla were nowhere to be found.

"Where is everybody? It's my birthday."

Mom tossed me a hot blackened muffin. "Your sisters are doing me a couple favors and your dad's still in bed."

I couldn't believe it. "Still in bed? It's so late!"

Mom found her keys and my book bag and scooted me toward the door. "Everybody will be here when you get back. Now come on! We're gonna be late."

"But I have to see Dad before I go. He loves wishing me happy birthday."

Mom nudged me toward the garage. "He'll tell you when we get back. Let's go."

I gave up and got in the car and then I remembered I still needed my scarf.

We were only at the mailbox. "Mom, we have to go back. I forgot my scarf."

"There's no time, Maggie. We're already late."

"But I need it! I can't write without it."

"Honey, it's July. The last thing you need is a scarf."

"But I never do anything without that scarf. DO YOU WANT ME TO FAIL?"

She kept driving. "No, I don't want you to fail. That's why I'm trying to get you there on time!"

I begged and begged, but she wouldn't budge and all of a sudden we were at the library and she was shoving me out of the car and I couldn't believe she was really doing this to me ON MY BIRTHDAY.

"We're not even late! Why can't we just go back? Dad can say happy birthday and I can get my scarf. I'll be so fast, I swear!"

"Come on, Maggie," Mom pleaded. "Don't let this ruin your birthday."

I could feel myself losing it. "Why are you trying to get rid of me?! Why can't I just see Dad?"

"Tell you what, if I see your scarf when I get home, I'll bring it back to you."

I swallowed my sniffles and pushed the hot tears out of my eyes. "You promise?"

She held up her hand. "I swear on your sister."

"Which one?"

"Layla."

I thought about it for a second. "Okay, I trust you."

When I came into the library, the arctic air made me shiver and I got mad all over again. I needed my scarf for more than writing, I needed it to protect me from hypothermia! I took a seat next to an older woman who smelled like mothballs and peppermint. There were four other women in the class but no men because men aren't in touch with their feelings.

The camp leader was a woman named Margot. She had short brown hair that swooped in all kinds of weird directions. She was small, but on the chubby side of small, and she must've seen the goose bumps on my arms because she offered me her sweater, but I politely declined. I wasn't ready for anyone to be nice to me. I was still too mad.

Margot talked about our class and our goals and our assignment, which was to write a piece of fiction inspired by a real event and some other stuff, but I didn't hear any of it because my mind was racing at ludicrous speed. Why couldn't we have turned around? Why didn't Dad want to see me ON MY BIRTHDAY? Why was Mom always pushing me off like I was some kind of chore? How come every time Layla or Tiffany needed something, everyone dropped everything to get it? Didn't anyone care about me?

My face flushed with hot and I asked to go to the bathroom. Margot said I could go whenever I wanted and didn't have to ask.

I went into the first stall and just sat there for a few minutes thinking and thinking and thinking. Finally, I came out, splashed water on my face, and looked in the mirror. There were big red angry splotches on my neck. Even my neck was mad that my scarf wasn't wrapped around it.

I took a few deep breaths and decided to pull it together because this was a once-in-a-lifetime opportunity. I walked back out into the library, where I saw Margot talking to a new girl. Great, just when I thought

I had the competition beat a new girl showed up. Could this day get any worse? As I got closer, I realized it wasn't a new girl at all.

It was Layla.

At first I thought Mom had sent her with my scarf but the only thing in her hands were car keys. And they were shaking.

"What are you doing here?"

She looked at me and suddenly I was scared. Her face was streaked with mascara. "Maggie, it's Dad. He's in the hospital."

A pit the size of the Grand Canyon filled my stomach. I grabbed her hand and we ran out to the car and she drove really fast, which was against the law, but I didn't care. I asked her a million questions that she barely answered.

"What happened?"

"It was a seizure."

"Was Mom there?"

"No. She was on her way back from the library."

"Oh no. Was he alone?"

"No. Tiffany was there. She called 911."

"Oh God. An ambulance came?"

"Yes."

"Where's Tiffany now?"

"At the hospital with Mom."

"Is Dad going to be okay?"

(silence)

"IS DAD GOING TO BE OKAY?"

(silence)

"They.
Don't.
Know."

CHAPTER EIGHTEEN

I felt the splotches on my neck multiply by a million. We screeched into the only open space at the back of the hospital and ran across the parking lot and I sang the "Fifty Nifty United States" song in my head so my legs wouldn't stop running. Layla tugged my arm through the sliding doors, down hall after hall, past gown after gown, toward an elevator that BINGed and opened beneath a big sign that read, "Intensive Care Unit."

We found Mom and Tiffany sitting on a waiting room bench. I wanted to run into Mom's arms but her hands had a death grip on a piece of tissue that she was twisting superhumanly tight. She didn't even notice us until I sat down right next to her and asked, "Where's Dad?" She turned her hazel eyes toward me. Right now they were more red than green.

"Oh Maggie, how was camp? Did you get a good assignment?"

I pulled the tissue from her hands and stared at her. "Is Dad okay?" And suddenly, I broke down into sobs, which Mayfields don't do because we always pull up our bootstraps, but I couldn't reach them. Not this time.

Tiffany grabbed my arm and yanked me into the hallway and I started hiccup crying, and although it's a little different, Mayfields really aren't supposed to do that either.

Tiffany knelt next to me and shook both my shoulders. "Pull it together. You're upsetting Mom."

I couldn't catch my breath. "I don't want . . . Dad . . . to die."

She shook me again. "Stop it. He's not gonna die!"

"What happened?"

She looked away. "He wasn't feeling well this morning so Mom made me call the doctor and then she left with you and I went to check on him and he wouldn't wake up. So I called 911. Mom got there just when the ambulance did and he started shaking and—"

I shook my head. "I don't think I'm supposed to know any of this."

Tiffany wouldn't let me go. "You need to know this stuff, Maggie. You're not a little kid anymore!"

I yanked my arm away as hard as I could yank and yelled, "YES. I. AM."

Tiffany yelled at me to grow up and I yelled at her to leave me alone and then I ran. I ran and ran. I ran down the hallway, past gown after scary gown, into the elevator, down to the lobby, and out the door, where I collapsed on the pavement. Maybe I should have prayed. But I knew better. If a church didn't have room for our prayers, no way did a hospital.

I was crying a scary amount and I worried I might have depleted my body's water to around 40% of its usual 80%. Why should I grow up? Every time I tried to grow up I found out they were hiding stuff from me. Important stuff. And every time I asked for the truth Dad told me to wait ten years and Mom told me I wouldn't understand.

But I wanted to understand. I knew I couldn't fix Dad. No one could. But I wanted to know why all of this was happening to my family. To my dad.

I wanted to know why he said bad things didn't happen to good looking people but then they kept happening to us. I wanted to know why every time they convinced me something wasn't a big deal it turned into an even bigger deal. I wanted to know if things would have been differ- ent if I had been there. If we had just turned around to get my scarf, if I could have just seen Dad, I could have saved him. I could have held his hand so he wasn't hold- ing his own. I could have gotten him a popsicle. I could have stopped him from shaking.

I started hyperventilating. I tried to stand up but I fell back to my knees. And then someone picked me up.

Mom carried me like she used to when I fell asleep in the car. I put my arms around her neck like I was five years old again. She sat me down on a bench, and then she knelt in front of me and pushed my tear-soaked hair out of my hot face. I tried to talk but she just whispered, "Shh. Shh."

Finally I calmed down enough to ask, "Is Dad okay?"

"Still haven't heard anything."

"Would you tell me if you had?"

"I'm going to tell you a story. Did I ever tell you about my mom?"

She hadn't. I knew she died when Mom was really little so I never asked about her. I don't know why. I guess to me, she hadn't really existed. I shook my head no and she went on.

"My mom was tall like Tiffany and kind like Layla and smart just like you. And she made dinner every night. And she sat on the porch while I caught fireflies. And she read me bedtime stories and then when I was eight, she died. And my childhood was over. My dad didn't know how to cook and clean so I learned how to do it. I did my homework and then I did housework. I made my first Thanksgiving dinner when I was nine. I was a grown-up before my time and I didn't realize how much fun being young could be until I met your father. He just kind of lit up my life and we went on adventures.

"And that is what I want for you, Maggie. I want you to have adventures. I want you to squeeze every ounce out of the time you have right now."

I didn't know what to say, which was weird because I always had something to say.

She scooted up right next to me. "Your dad is sick. Very sick. But he is going to get better. And when he does, we're going to have a Maggie birthday do-over."

I squeezed her tight. I didn't want a birthday do-over. I wanted my dad.

We went back up to the waiting room where it was minus one hundred degrees. I nuzzled in close to Mom's side again because it was warm there because her body functioned at a temperature higher than most adults because she had more to do than anyone else.

She winked at my sisters. "You know your father, he loves making a scene. But don't worry, girls. Everything's going to be okay."

I felt safe next to her molten side. And I believed her. I believed her because when Mom said everything was going to be fine then everything would be fine because Mom did everything 100% which meant her promises were 100%. At least from now on.

Mom reached into her bag and dug around for a few seconds. When she found what she was looking for, she presented it in a big ta-da.

It was my scarf.

She wrapped it around my neck. "It was in the car. You must've left it when we went to see the fireworks." She was right. She was always right. She'd kept the scarf promise 100%, which made me believe even more that Dad would be okay.

The next couple of hours were the longest hours in the history of hours. Mom was the only one allowed to see Dad and she would disappear for a few minutes and then come back and then disappear into the bathroom for a few minutes and then come back with a new tissue to twist even tighter. And each time she'd say, "Nothing new yet."

I couldn't get comfortable in the waiting room because the chairs were made of rocks covered in ugly mauve fabric. I tried to read a magazine but they were all at least three months old. And I tried to watch TV but it was all reruns. I swear the whole place felt like it was on pause, including us. Nothing could happen until Dad was okay.

Layla and Tiffany were anxiously bouncing their legs up and down. If Dad had been there, he would have said, "Turn your motors off." But Dad wasn't there. He was in a hospital room, all alone, wearing a gown we all knew he'd hate because cool dudes don't wear dresses. I listened to the clock tick then tock and we just kind of sat there. In silence. Waiting for someone to tell us something. Other families filed in and out in varying degrees of upset. But none of them stayed as long as we did because no one loved anyone as much as we loved Dad.

Tiffany got up to pace in the hall and Mom disappeared into the bathroom again and Layla and I just sat there in the most silent of silence. I hadn't been alone with her since the car and before that I hadn't been alone with her since my student of the month breakfast. She looked really worried, like more worried than the rest of us. I felt we could both use a laugh so I finally broke the silence.

"Man, I could really use a cigarette."

She laughed and sniffed. "What?"

"I don't know. That's what they say in the movies when something really intense is happening."

Layla shook her head. "In what movie does that happen, Maggie?"

"I can't think of one exactly, but I swear I've heard it before. Maybe I read it in a book. It sounds like something they would say in *The Great Gatsby*." I gave myself a 1920s gangster accent and said, "Yeah, you see doll, I could really use a cigarette."

Layla laughed again and then tried not to. "We shouldn't be laughing."

"Why not?"

"Because this is scary."

"Why are you so scared? You know more than the rest of us."

She came over and sat next me and I immediately felt weird. Layla never voluntarily sat next to me. Even at the dinner table, my chair was way on the other end. Plus, I was scared she'd smell her perfume, which I'd sprayed all over my body before I'd left the house.

"I know you're upset with Mom and Dad for not telling you everything that's been going on." Her eyes welled with tears. "But I swear, as much as you wish you knew more, I double wish that I knew less."

You know how in *Sleeping Beauty*, the prince kisses the princess and she wakes up? Well at least, I hear that's how it happened. I don't like seeing kissing so I always look away at that part. But that's kind of how I felt when Layla said what she did. A kiss didn't shake me out of sleep. Her words did.

And I hadn't even realized I'd been asleep. Metaphorically asleep. Figuratively in the dark about one huge thing: All that was happening wasn't just happening to me. It was happening to all five of us. And all of us were scared. All of us were confused. And none of us knew what was going to happen next. But that didn't stop Layla from taking care of Dad every morning and being Mom when Mom didn't have time to be Mom. And it didn't stop Mom from working so hard so much both at work and at home. And while Tiffany was mostly a jerk, at the same time she was mostly brave especially for calling 911 when she did. And Dad, geez, Dad. He was fighting with all his might. Not just for him. But for all of us.

I realized I hadn't been alone in my mission. All five of us were trying to fix Dad.

At that moment, Mom burst back in through the doors. "Maggie! It's still your birthday!"

I wiped the tears from my eyes. "Just for a couple more hours."

Tiffany came back just in time to roll her eyes. "Um, you did get fifteen whole days before today."

"Fourteen. Today doesn't count."

Mom reached into her bag again. "Well, I brought one of your presents. I meant to give it to you before your class, but—" She handed me the package and I felt more TERRIBLE than I have ever felt in my life.

I felt TERRIBLE as a rush of remembering reminded me of the big deal I'd made out of my scarf before. I looked away. "I don't deserve any gifts. I'm a horrible, horrible person."

"That's what I've been saying all along!" Tiffany said.

Mom shot her a death stare and sat next to me on the bench. "Of course you deserve it. Here, open it."

I unpeeled the wrapping paper and pulled out the most beautiful leather-bound journal I'd ever seen. It smelled old and new at the same time and the pages were yellow like the paper the Declaration of Independence was written on. This paper was clearly for big deal writing.

I pushed it away. "I can't take this. It's too nice."

Mom pushed it back. "Exactly. You need a really nice journal to write your memoir in."

This was the single best gift I'd ever received on the single worst day of my entire life. I hugged the journal close and then I hugged Mom and then I went to hug Tiffany but then I remembered that I hated her.

Mom gave Layla change for the vending machine and she bought us four Otis Spunkmeyer cookies, which were DELICIOUS. Mom asked around the waiting room to see if anyone had matches and an old man with a pipe let her have one of his, so she struck it, stuck it in my cookie, and told me to make a wish.

I closed my eyes, took a deep breath, and wished for Dad to be okay. And it worked! An hour later, the nurse came and got us.

We all walked down the hall through two giant doors and down another hall. Mom held my hand and covered my eyes as we walked past a scary row of rooms. But even though I couldn't see, I could still smell the serious sick coming from inside. When we got to Dad's room, Mom uncovered my eyes, pulled back the curtain, and there he was.

Dad smiled. "I need a cocktail."

Layla ran for his neck, Tiffany ran for his waist, and I ran for his legs because it was the only place left to run to.

He wiggled what he could wiggle. "Come on, girls. What are you trying to do? Kill me?"

Tiffany punched him in the stomach. "Not funny!"

Dad pushed us all away. "Everyone, calm down. I'm fine."

I looked around the room: beeping machines, dripping bags, needles taped to his arms. He didn't *look* fine.

The doctor came in a few minutes later and told us what had happened. Dad had gotten an infection that turned into a bigger infection that had caused a seizure. They had him on all the right medicines now, but he'd have to stay at least a week to get the full round of drugs that he needed.

"There's nothing to worry about," the doctor promised. "This is just what happens as the disease progresses. But we know how to treat this part."

Dad squeezed my hand and said, "Doc, at least tell me you can get me medical marijuana."

The doctor laughed but quickly became a doctor again and sternly said, "No."

Then Dad got really tired so we went back to the waiting room so he could get some rest. It was way past all of our bedtimes.

Mom dug around in her purse for her keys. "You girls go home. I'll stay here with Dad."

Layla crossed her arms. "We're not going anywhere, Mom."

"Yeah." Tiffany nodded. "As long as Dad's here, we're here."

I got kind of excited. "We can build a blanket fort!"

Mom shook her head. "No. Just go home and get some rest. You can come back first thing in the morning."

Layla refused. "No way, Mom."

Tiffany did too. "We're not leaving you in this scary place."

"Yeah, lady," I said. "We're like the Five Musketeers.[63] All for one and one for all."

Mom finally caved. "Okay, go home and get what you need. Then come back and we'll figure something out."

As soon as we got home, we rushed inside and grabbed everything we needed. I went to the pantry first and got the necessities. Little Debbies. Fruit snacks. Granola bars. Then I went to the fridge and found juice boxes and a bottle of mixer just in case Dad was serious about that cocktail. Layla took sleeping bags and Tiffany took pillows and I packed my PJs, a couple changes of clothes, and a few hundred pens.

But when Layla and I were ready to go, Tiffany was nowhere to be found. I went into Dad's bathroom and found her sobbing over the sink, hugging a bottle of Listerine.

Okay, I have to admit: At first, I was kind of relieved to see her crying. I felt like it gave me permission to do it too. But as soon as she saw me, her sobs turned to yells and she ordered me to leave.

---

63. Oh wow a 5 Musketeers sounds like a way better candy bar than a 3 Musketeers. I'm imagining extra nougat. Lots and lots of extra nougat.

I didn't leave. I stood there cautiously like I was standing in front of an angry bear that might charge me at any second. Since I didn't have any honey, I tried to calm her down with words. "Mom says everything's going to be okay."

Tiffany was opening every drawer, looking for something. "Dad needs floss. Do you see any floss?" Dad didn't floss and she knew it.

"Dad doesn't floss," I said carefully.

She slammed a drawer. "Well, he should! His teeth are going to rot out of his head!" She slammed more drawers like a crazy person.

"Tiffany, stop, you're freaking me out."

"*You're* freaked out? You weren't even here! You didn't even see him!"

"Stop it! You're scaring me!"

Her eyes filled with more angry tears. "Good! Now you know how I felt!"

Layla came in and glared at us both. "Stop it, you two. Come on. Mom needs us."

We walked back out through Mom and Dad's room and I saw what I'd missed on the way in: Dad's favorite Eric Clapton shirt ripped to pieces on the floor. Stretcher wheel marks in the carpet. Needle caps everywhere. And Dad's wheelchair waiting for him next to the TV.

Layla told us to go get in the car so we got in the car.

Tiffany immediately began fixing her makeup in the mirror. "Layla is taking this big sister thing way too far."

"No kidding," I agreed. "She's not the boss of us."

And just like that, Tiffany and I were back on neutral ground. Until the next masking tape line was drawn down the middle of our room.

Five minutes later, Layla appeared carrying Dad's folded-up wheelchair and a giant bag of Hershey's Kisses. And not to be mean, but she had crazy in her eyes.

Tiffany rolled down her window. "Um, what are you *doing*?"

Layla opened the back door and crammed the chair and the Kisses next to me. "Dad's going to need his chair eventually. And he loves Hershey's Kisses. I leave three for him to have after lunch every day."

Tiffany shook her head. "Well, it's a good thing you're bringing three thousand then."

I laughed. Tiffany's meanness was actually pretty entertaining when it wasn't directed at me.

We rode back to the hospital in silence. Tiffany hugged Dad's Listerine bottle while I sat as still as possible, not able to move a muscle because of Dad's chair. I couldn't even reach the Hershey's Kisses.

Back in the waiting room, Mom had built us a blanket fort on the floor and was asleep in Dad's room in the chair next to his bed.

Tiffany stretched out her giraffe legs and fell asleep almost instantly. I thought of the disaster in Mom and Dad's room and hoped she was going to dream about something good, like being crowned Homecoming Queen or Prom Queen or whatever other kind of queen hot girls get crowned in high school.

Layla fell asleep next. It was weird seeing her because even in her sleep, she looked perfect. And she didn't look crazy or scared, not even a little.

When Mom came in to check on us I didn't want her to worry, so I pretended I was asleep too. She leaned over and kissed my forehead.

"Good night, Maggie." Busted.

I opened an eye and looked at her leaning over us. I could see every freckle on her tired face. "Good night, Mom," I whispered.

The next morning I was the last one up. Mom must've already had a bazillion cups of coffee because she was buzzing with energy.

"Good morning sunshine."

"Good morning." I yawned. "How's Dad?"

She picked up my pillow. "Well, there's nothing on TV, his butt hurts from sleeping on that hard bed, and his hair looks terrible. But other than that, he's much better. Wanna go see him?"

I nodded yes, pulled on my shoes, and walked through the maze to his room, blindfolded by Mom's hand.

Sunlight glared through the blinds and painted lines across Dad's face. He poked at a bowl of Jell-O with a fork.

"You gonna eat that?"

He pushed it toward me. "It's all yours."

I took a closer look at the bowl of Jell-O. It was orange, not red. "Nah, I only like the red kind."

"Me too."

Mom went into the hall to talk to the nurse and left me alone with Dad. I thought it was going to be weird to be alone with him, but it wasn't. Despite all the machines and bags and smells, he was still just Dad.

We talked about politics and music and why red Jell-O was better than orange Jell-O[64] and then Mom reappeared with my book bag.

"Your sisters and I are going down to the cafeteria. Want to come?"

I almost said yes until I saw Dad's face. He looked so down and I knew I couldn't leave him alone, even if I was dying for some red Jell-O. He'd been alone in that cold and terrible room long enough.

So I stayed and made myself comfortable in the world's most uncomfortable chair. When I took out my new leather journal, Dad smiled.

---

64. Because orange tastes too much like oranges.

"Oh good. She gave it to you. You know, I picked that out myself."

I turned back the cover to the first page and wrote my name. "Did you really pick it out?"

"Actually, your mother did. But it was my idea."

I gave him a look. "Was it really your idea?"

"No, but your mother gets credit for everything." He laughed his cool guy laugh that usually made me feel better.

But right then, I didn't feel better. Which I didn't understand, because if Dad was feeling better then so should I, right? I wasn't sick. I didn't have scary things in my arms and nose.

But I felt terrible. I felt lost. Dad looked different to me now.

Sure, his face was the same, just with more stubble. And his eyes were still blue, just a little less bright. But he was hard to recognize and not just because he wasn't wearing a rock 'n' roll T-shirt.

Dad had always said he was an adventurer. A dreamer. Which made his new state of sick all the more terrible. It was like he was a free spirit who was no longer free.

I felt like begging him to tell me everything was going to be okay. That he was going to be okay. I needed to hear it from him. I needed to know he was going to be there for every single important thing. I needed him to hear my speech as high school valedictorian where I planned on quoting Abraham Lincoln[65] and Neil Young.[66] I needed him to be there for every single victory. Every single prize whether it be Nobel, Pulitzer, or Cracker Jack.

I needed my dad back. The adventurer. The dreamer. The free spirit.

He cleared his throat. "Hey Mags." I looked up at him and he took a deep breath. Every single blanket piled on top of him rose and then fell with his words. "I'm *really* sorry."

I thought about yelling. But I didn't.

I thought about crying. But I couldn't.

I thought about running away. But honestly, I was sick of running.

I thought about thinking. And how I needed to do more of it.

Even if that seemed impossible because I already thought so much. But I needed to change my thought trajectory to get closer to how I could help Dad. And Mom. And Layla. And maybe even Tiffany. And all that thinking led to one thought: Fixing Dad didn't have to just mean curing him. Fixing Dad could mean a million things. And right now it meant I should just be here for

---

65. "Always bear in mind that your own resolution to succeed is more important than any one thing."

66. That really deep thing he said about burning out, not fading away.

him. Even though I was so many adjectives like scared, sad, confused, tired, and yes, even hungry. I should also be one more adjective.

I should be brave.

So I stood and pulled up my bootstraps. I reached up to him and wrapped my scarf around his neck. And then I said to him the four words I so desperately wanted him to say to me.

"Dad—it's gonna be okay."

His face was confident even though his voice was shaking. "It's definitely gonna be okay, Mags."

The rush of hospital cold hit my neck and I went back to the chair and back to the open book waiting for me. Right now seemed like as good a time as any to start my very first chapter. But my mind went blank.

"I'm not really sure what to write. What do you think?"

Dad took a long sip of juice and thought about it. "Well, I think you're supposed to write what you know. So what do you know?"

That sounded too daunting. I knew way too many things. It would be impossible to narrow them down.

I held the book for a minute and thought about it. "What would you write about?"

He gathered all of his thoughts and thoughtfully said, "I'll tell you in ten years."

I pictured what we would be like ten years from that moment. I was going to know so much about Dad that I could write a whole book just about him. I would know all of his inside jokes and I would know what the hippies wrote in shaving cream on his car on his wedding day and I would know every single Neil Young song, even the B-sides, bootlegs, and rarities. I would know so many other things that he would finally tell me in ten years.

But right now, I could only write what I knew RIGHT NOW. So I uncapped my pen and wrote the first thing that popped into my head.

Beep.

Beep.

Beep.

My dad won't stop beeping.

ACKNOWLEDGMENTS

My mother is a big believer in thank yous. So here we go.

Thank you to my super agent Marietta Zacker for seeing something in this story long before there was anything to see. I'm not sure why the universe spun you in my direction but I'm so very grateful that she did. I look forward to sharing many more stories with you wrapped in red ribbons.

Thank you to my big deal editor Ginee Seo for pushing me with all her might. You make me unbelievably nervous, which makes me work harder, dig deeper, and eat snacks I shouldn't. Thank you for being unmerciful.

Thank you Taylor Norman for being my Crow Family. Our cosmic connection is strong and hopefully even after you reach the very top, you can still hear me ka-kaaing from down below.

Thank you Amelia Mack and Anja Mulder for putting all your talent, gumption, and goodwill into our cover. Thank you Julie Romeis for first bringing me into the Chronicle family. And thank you to the Chronicle family for making me one of your very own. 680 Second Street definitely houses the most talented brains and eyeballs this side of the galaxy.

Thank you to my family for letting me tell our story. Thank you to my mom. You're terrible at cutting bangs but you're an incredibly cool, strong, courageous, and beautiful woman. I hope I'm just like you when I grow up. Thank you to my sister Rayna for answering my desperate phone calls. You're always so encouraging and helpful even while your children are screaming in the background. I totally get why you were Dad's favorite. Thank you to my sister Alison for paying me ten dollars every time you skipped school. We could not be more different. And not just in bra size. But I love you. No matter how many times you lock me out of our room.

Thank you to my brave husband, Ted. You always said I would fall head over heels in love with you after this book was finally finished. But the truth is I've been madly in love with you since you sat on the floor of Elegant Mr. Gallery and showed me your Micro Machines collection so many moons ago. I've just been playing it cool ever since. I look forward to a lifetime of pizza eating contests with you.

Thank you to my dear and bearded friend Rob Calabro who gave me the gumption to collect my memories into something more. You are truly the most talented person I know. I would hate you if I didn't admire you so much. Thank you Alexa, well, for every single thing. It's official, you're the nicest. Thank you, Cyndi Harvell, for scoring the sound track to this book and the life that inspired it. And my warmest gratitude to the handful of friends and family who have read this story along the way. I will return the favor in hugs and milkshakes. Except for Schermer, I owe you pie. And Julie, I owe you frozen yogurt. And Jess, I owe you cheese.

And finally thank you to my dad. While you live on in Ty, Lane, Mac, Brady, Drew, and hopefully many more grandchildren to come, your incredible fight lives on in these pages. I miss you. I love you. And I hope that one day we will once again watch *The Wonder Years* together while sharing Oreos. You get the cream side.

DISCUSSION QUESTIONS FOR
THE MEANING OF MAGGIE

1. How does Mr. Mayfield's multiple sclerosis profoundly impact and change the lives of each of his family members? Do you think they are ultimately better people because of what happens to him?

2. In what ways does Mr. Mayfield's poor relationship with his own parents impact his philosophy regarding family relationships? Do you think his method of parenting would be different had he not had this experience?

3. How is Maggie's relationship with her father different than her relationship with her mother? Do you find her to be closer to one of them than the other? Do you happen to have a parent with whom you are closer? If so, why?

4. Consider the cover art for *The Meaning of Maggie*. In what ways are these objects symbolic of the events that transpire throughout the course of the book?

5. When Maggie asks Tiffany if she looks different on her birthday, Tiffany tells her, "Yeah. You look even nerdier than you did yesterday." How is Tiffany's comment indicative of their relationship? How does Maggie's relationship with each of her sisters change throughout the course of the novel?

6. Why does Maggie choose to keep her science fair topic secret from her family? Do you think she is right to do so? What do you think she fears will happen if they know the truth?

7. What is Clyde's appeal for Maggie? Though he seems impressed by Maggie, ultimately he sends a Flower-Gram to Mary Winter; why do you think he chooses her over Maggie?

8. In considering her earlier successes with resolutions, Maggie decides that she can and will fix her dad. Why is her strategy so ambitious? What is the danger in having such a plan?

9. When Maggie learns her family has kept her father's treatment from her, do you feel her strong reaction is warranted? In your opinion, did they make the right decision? Why or why not?

10. *The Meaning of Maggie* is told from Maggie's point of view; how would the story be different if another Mayfield were telling it?

11. Why does Layla ask for help from Maggie on her homework assignment for *To Kill a Mockingbird*?

12. Consider the characters in *The Meaning of Maggie*. Who did you like the most? The least? For what reason? Of all of the characters, who did you feel was most similar to you due to his or her personality or experiences?

13. How does Maggie's opinion about Mary Winter change throughout the course of the novel? What does she learn from their running experiences?

14. In the prologue of *The Meaning of Maggie*, Maggie, who aspires to be president of the United States, offers her rationale for writing a memoir of her year. She states, "So maybe I didn't cut down a cherry tree and maybe I don't have wooden teeth and I wasn't born in a log cabin with a dirt floor and nine thousand brothers and sisters. I still have something to say." In your opinion, why is Maggie's story so important? How does her telling it help her deal with the challenges in her world? What essential story about your life would you like to tell?